LED ASTRAY

A CRIME THRILLER

BOOK 1 OF THE AVIA CHRONICLES

KARLIANNA VONCIL

TCK PUBLISHING.COM

ISBN: 978-1-63161-059-2

Published by TCK Publishing
www.TCKpublishing.com

Get discounts and special deals on books at
www.TCKpublishing.com/bookdeals

Get in touch with Karlianna and find out more at
www.karliannavoncil.com

For Daddy—first one is yours

PART ONE

O
N A WEDNESDAY NIGHT, THE third of the month, they discovered the body after a woman called in and said she'd found her dog chewing on a human hand.

The body had been retrieved at exactly 4:32 in the morning. The neighborhood was well-known to the officers—just two months prior, the Channel 5 news team had filmed them live as they broke into a house where an accused murderer had been hiding. As they dragged him out, forty-two years old, naked and cursing at them in a mixture of Spanish and English, one of the officers had snapped at the camera crew for getting too close—so close that he'd run headfirst into the news team's equipment as they wrestled the suspect into the squad car. The footage, complete with his own colorful language, had been replayed at least seven times the next day.

Detectives Martinez and van Daan surveyed the neighborhood, trying to see what hadn't already been seen. The neighborhood and countless others had been canvassed months before when the disappearance had been fresh and media hype over the missing girl had reached its dizzying frenzy. They had turned up next to nothing week after week, and eventually all the usual concerns—burglaries, armed robberies, the occasional violent suicide—had pressed in until they took precedence, and the weeks that stretched between the missing report and their last good lead had reached uncomfortable lengths.

Until now, now that she'd finally been unearthed.

There were at least two separate households on the block watching them, Detective Martinez noted. People were wary of cops in this part of town. "As well they should be," van Daan had said, leisurely buttoning his vest. "Pick any random person out of that part of town and they'll either be a bum, an addict, or a welfare case. Crime is practically in the water here."

Van Daan, having also spotted the figures lurking in windows, waved at them jauntily and stared until the windows had been covered again. For his part, Martinez ignored them. He was watching the people behind the yellow tape in their protective gear, taking pictures and notes with latex-gloved hands. He listened to their chatter, tried to hone in on phrases he anticipated, waited anxiously for anything surprising. The paramedics had gotten the signal to arrive on scene, which had been a waste of time: The victim had crossed the last threshold months ago.

The hand they'd recovered had been dug up by a white miniature chihuahua named Killer who had already ingested part of the index finger and snapped viciously at the team when he'd been handed off by the owner.

"We'll have to get back the part the mutt ate," van Daan said, and a few others murmured disapproval. Martinez ignored that also. He wanted to see the body.

The girl had been buried in a shallow grave behind a dumpster in an area shaded by two gnarled, emaciated elm trees and littered with trash and debris. The ground, hardened by an early autumn frost, did not yield her easily. The clothes she'd died in had not been thrown away, but clung stubbornly to the flesh. She'd been wrapped in a bed sheet, originally baby blue with yellow-and-white stars. The blue of the fabric was bleached near-white, the stars splotched and distorted; the team hashed forensics, trying to gauge what they could from the stains. There were the thin tendrils of mottled brown hair hanging off the skull like limp seaweed; there were the patches of skin and unknown residue tattooed on the surface; her blank, washed-out blue eyes still witnessing a spectacle they could not fathom.

On the night she died, their victim had been wearing jeans and a pink blouse so sheer it was little more than a blushing veil. The scant sensuality of her black lace underwear was almost grotesque. She'd worn a pair of black stilettos, and a cross pendant huddled in the hollow of her throat on a chain of sterling silver. No purse or bag was recovered; the police assumed that her cellphone and wallet were disposed of and didn't expect to retrieve them.

To Martinez's left, van Daan was talking quietly and assuredly. "Put the tape up over and along there…yes, we'll need to call the family and tell them to come up to the station…what? Yes, now, the number is…what? Yeah, go ahead and call the Chief, tell him… No, no press, Jesus Christ, not until we have a chance to… honestly, have them crawling out of our asses before we can even get a statement…"

Martinez paid him no mind. He watched the team unravel the tape, enveloped by the orchestra of voices and cameras and phone calls. The cue he awaited would come later. So much prep work had to get done before the real work could begin; he was almost desperate for the autopsy to hurry up and confirm the cause of death.

He waited long enough for the crews to get started before he moved past the tape and started his own hunt. It was habit by now; most of the time he found nothing, but as told van Daan when he noticed and complained—which was almost always—he was never really sure what was significant at a crime scene until he'd picked through it himself.

And today was special. Today he actually found something. He watched the antiseptic light of the squad car's headlights and the workers' flashlights shift around him—and suddenly he noticed a metallic glint in the brush nearby. He dropped to his knees and dug with one hand.

It was a makeup compact, green, with pink and blue rhinestones decorating the lid in the shape of a heart. Someone had wedged it in the underbrush. The search team, here only for an hour or so, had been meticulous in their turnover. The object couldn't have been there before that.

Martinez hesitated, then pocketed the compact. He had a hunch forming, but as he had very little else to support the idea, there was no need to bag and tag it; van Daan and the chief would not penalize him for it. After a moment's consideration, he carefully climbed over the tape without looking back.

After dismissing the medics and contacting the lab, he found van Daan on the other side of the lot warning an elderly woman with a Polaroid to back the hell up and, "Show some goddamn respect, lady. The girl is dead." Martinez clapped a hand on his shoulder and turned him away.

"Come on," he said. "The Chief is waiting."

Sweet Valley was a town of no less than one hundred thousand, set on the main highway and complete with all the trappings of a big city. There was a civic center, a newly reconstructed opera hall, a mall, and a slew of company headquarters and their official bases. There was also a ghost of a caste system firmly entrenched: the average citizen—were he touring the sun-scorched plateaus of the Texas Panhandle—would see neighborhoods of east and south Sweet Valley flourishing with green manicured lawns and luxurious shrubbery. The closest markets were organic grocers, and the schools boasted champion athletics and state-attested excellence. Going west and then north began the descent; the grass began to wither, the trees thinned where they hunched on private lawns, and there were no joggers loping down the sidewalks. There were stores and schools adorned with iron bars and neighborhood-advocacy signs. From the town's summit, the overpass unfurled, cornered by an abandoned hospital and a foreclosed packing company. And in the valley below lay Pleasantville.

Pleasantville, though considered an integrated section of the city, was a small town unto itself nestled in the rolling hills. Here the Texas Panhandle, golden and green and unassuming, became an afterthought. The roads dipped and swayed, became earthen and dark in certain places. Very few regularly tread these grounds. Their star attraction was the town's only amusement park, which included the fairgrounds that hosted all the local trade shows. The county fair drifted in faithfully every September. The trash and human waste hitchhiked on the winds from the north and flooded the rest of the city with the ugly, sticky, unwelcome reminders of their existence.

Even before the discovery of Emily Burns's body in the heart of the valley, Pleasantville had been forced to open its ranks to the inquisitions of the rest of the population because of its substantial—and steadily growing—numbers of registered sex offenders. But such a revelation surprised no one. In the 1980s, it was revealed that, after the capturing, indicting, trialing, and condemning had been concluded, the state's twenty-ninth confirmed serial rapist had been born and bred in those dimly lit streets. Local runaways disappeared then reappeared in crack-houses and makeshift brothels. Mandatory neighborhood watches were promised to be regulated and investigated on a case-by-case basis by the city officials. This was promised not for the citizens of Pleasantville, but for the society outside, who wished to see the slimy underbelly of their city effectively contained.

For their own part, the people of Pleasantville were amiable enough, but only in passing and only to their own. Constant police vigilance and scrutiny from outsiders had pushed Pleasantville to adopt suspicion and anonymity as tools of their daily trade, and while the illicit drugs and illegal activities found a ready haven in their hills, these crimes were uncovered with equal parts gratitude and resentment. The discovery of Emily offered more proof that Pleasantville was little more than a playground for monsters.

Emily was the only child of Elizabeth and Edward Burns. The Burns family had paid their pound of flesh to Sweet Valley—at least fourteen generations' worth. The Burns family had thick veins running through the local medical field—five Burns men had pursued careers as doctors, including Emily's father. Dr. Edward Burns III had been a Marine studying biology at the same time Elizabeth had been a cheerleader studying education. The couple met at a group study session their sophomore year of college. In the Burns's dining hall, a story takes place in portraits: on the left wall, in a stark black frame to outset the golden sunset paint, is a photo of Elizabeth's silhouette, her back to the camera as Edward proposes. It's interesting, Elizabeth likes to say at dinner parties, that they chose that photo to commemorate the moment of their engagement. They'd had over a dozen to choose from, but none of the other shots had managed to catch the flash of Elizabeth's hair in the breeze; or the startled joy of her hands, flung out in front of her, extended out as if to clutch at her new fiancé; or even the unadulterated affection running like a current in the young Edward crouched before his bride.

"And besides," Elizabeth always adds, "you can see the Eiffel Tower in that particular shot so well."

The next photo is Emily at seven, cradling a handful of crushed flowers in her arms. As with so many typical childhood photos, she is missing a front tooth and the camera is tilted to show her gummy smile. The last image is a painted family portrait that catches the eye from its placement centered on the wall. Looking to the future, the Burns had left more space on the family wall, waiting to capture more moments. With the family wall behind them, the Burns dressed immaculately and sat at their dining table saying, "Please, we will do anything, anything at all, the number to contact is…" The footage was aired on every news station for three weeks; and of course, the Burns's photographs were splashed across every newspaper, at the ready for any mention of Emily, in every corner of the city.

Of all the photos taken at the crime scene, Detective Martinez took one and carried it on his person at all times: the one of Emily after she'd been completely dug up, laid out carefully on the ground and looking like she were a contraption that still needed assembling. Her parents gave him one of her posing on her front lawn in a pink mermaid prom gown, complete with rhinestones and a tiara. Another photo of her body laid out on the sterile metal sheet at the morgue sat on his desk. This and other photos, such as one of Emily sitting in front of her bedroom vanity applying mascara and smiling from the mirror's reflection, were lent to him from Emily's friends, and he knew where they are at all times as well. It was Emily's prom photo that, prior to her discovery, had been blown up on ten billboards across town—including the only one in Pleasantville.

Other families might have done much more in the public eye to bring their child home, but Martinez marveled at the couple's boldness. At the height of the frenzy surrounding their daughter's disappearance, they had been courted by major news stations and shows like *Inside Edition and Good Morning, America*, all of which they politely declined. A lawyer had appeared once on the six o'clock news on the family's behalf; his statement aired on television and was reprinted word for word in the Sunday paper, and that was all the Burnses had to say on the matter. Mr. Burns still went to work, and the couple attended church regularly. The Chief once remarked that one of Pleasantville's most outstanding families were trying to project a sense of normalcy with such tenacity that they were practically pretending their daughter never existed, but

Martinez disagreed. To him, the couple's absence from the airwaves and their attorney's clipped, pointed speech was pride; their quiet, hurried walk in public without eye contact or greetings was shame; and when he saw that photos and portraits of Emily were polished daily and still prominently displayed throughout the house, Martinez saw grief. That they were forced to suffer this loss and still maintain such a façade was just circumstance.

Emily died from a single gunshot wound to the face. The autopsy reported that the killer had shot her at close range; the bullet went through her left cheek and exited out the back of her skull. She had died instantly, which was a comfort to the officers and staff involved; not so much a comfort to Mr. and Mrs. Burns, who sat ramrod straight in the holding room, not touching or holding each other, and refused to break eye contact with Martinez as he delivered the news the way his training demanded. Even after finding the body and discovering the cause of death, there would still be more testing to do, more searching, interviewing, questioning and archiving all the files. He was quick to assure the couple that the utmost care and respect would be paid to Emily and that the body would be released to them as soon as possible.

That the department was doing everything within their power to find the killer and justice went without saying.

With the way the Burnses held themselves together during the meeting, Martinez marveled that they hadn't gotten a lawyer to come in and handle this conversation for them. But he didn't say this out loud. Instead, he finished up with the couple in the early afternoon and promptly went to touch base with the Chief.

Chief Hendricks was facing the end of a twenty-five-year career. There was a rumor that every time the Sweet Valley crime rate spiked, Hendricks shaved a few more days off his retirement countdown. His career had been no more challenging than any of his peers', but the past ten years had seen a strange and gradual shift. A shift in crime, yes—and in the criminals as well. A shift toward the sinister. It was all over the city. *Goddamn, but it's in the air already.* The Chief was a devout Baptist, and while everyone else had a scapegoat to blame, he insisted everyone was equally sick. The sickness was a gaping mouth, always begging to be fed, forever unsatisfied.

It was the sickness itself that let a girl like Emily get killed; that's what the Chief would say if Martinez asked.

The Chief was a tall, looming man with eagle-broad shoulders and a portly paunch that shook in a wave when he made long strides. He had salt-and-pepper hair and a stash of salt-and-pepper shakers in his office, with which he doctored his food at every meal he took at work.

He was digging into a microwave dinner disinterestedly when Martinez buzzed himself in.

"Did they take it okay?"

Martinez sat down. "As well as they can, I guess. They were cooperative."

"They've had some time to prepare." The Chief spooned mashed potatoes into his mouth. "I'll need you to talk to Penzley and see what they can get on the gun and the bullet."

Martinez shrugged. "We cleaned the area and emptied all the dumpsters three blocks around. It's unlikely we'll find anything out there. She was killed elsewhere, anyway."

"We still need to make the gesture. Did they contact the team over there in Wilton?"

"Wilton, sir?" Martinez watched the Chief stab half-frozen broccoli around on the tray. "Calling them might not even be necessary until we set up parameters for a new search."

"The news will have to be told sooner or later that we finally found the body and the case is up and running again. If we call Wilton, we can tell the stations we're putting feelers out there to launch a team. That there is how we set our parameters."

"Are we going to get a team together?"

"We might hold off on that. We're coming into this with a lot of time lost." The Chief dumped the remainder of the tray into the trash and cleared his throat. "Start with the parents. Give them a day or so, and then stop by and see if they can tell you anything new. Any extra person they can think of, anything the girl talked about—you talk to them. Get with van Daan and go back to the neighborhood, ask around to see if someone saw something."

They shook hands and Martinez exited, calling van Daan on the way to his car. He checked the time: 10:38 a.m. He had been awake for twenty-one hours.

As Martinez drove home to retire for the night, he couldn't help but notice four new billboards of Emily had been erected.

If anybody ever asked, Martinez would say he liked his job. At least he wasn't stuck behind a desk like some other officers he knew. At least he got to make a difference in people's lives.

What he wouldn't say is that on slow days, Martinez would see his crime victims as though they had never died, out of the corner of his eye, on street corners and in the doorways of homes he drove past. Always out of focus, always just out of frame. When a case was particularly gruesome, the longer it took to solve, the more he felt he was watched. Sometimes there was no other way to relieve the ache than to visit the site where it started and keep searching. By the time he had accepted in his mind that he wouldn't be getting any sleep that night, Martinez was already clipping his seatbelt on and backing down his driveway.

As he pulled out onto his street, he thought he saw Emily by the mailbox.

Someone had disturbed the yellow tape of the enclosure, and there was a new set of shoe prints that had yet to be documented, but Martinez catalogued this only in passing as he swept the grounds in a cursory motion. He searched diligently for fifteen minutes and reminded himself to document the time for his records. He righted himself from his crouch in the dead weeds.

He'd seen nothing else, but he was expecting that. He didn't get lucky every time, but that didn't stop him. All crime scenes looked basically the same after dark, anyway. So instead, Martinez focused on Emily. He felt he knew this victim, even though it had been only a few days now. Emily Burns, a young debutante, obviously seeking some connection that wouldn't be posted in a gilded frame and mounted on her family's dining room wall. In the frozen dirt and shredded wrappers, Martinez studied the earth and hoped the face of his perpetrator would peer out back to him.

Was it an older man? An older woman? From the way she was dressed, it was almost certain that she'd been with a lover. If Emily had been seeing someone she couldn't bring home, this was probably the neighborhood she'd find him in. But who was this stranger?

And where was he now?

As he walked back to his car, a chill October wind whipped through the street, washing cold air over Martinez. His pocket jangled—probably van

Daan asking about a fast food order, because he obviously wasn't finishing his paperwork at the station and wanted a distraction. He stopped himself and ignored the phone; van Daan would always call back. The entire block seemed gutted and hollow around him. Getting into the squad car and putting van Daan on speakerphone, he rolled out of the valley listening to his partner accost the drive-thru attendant as he ordered their dinner for the evening.

Interviewing the Burns had been a waste of time, as Martinez had guessed. The Burns were not outright hostile, but that wasn't necessary. It was in the way they did not reach out to shake or clasp his hands, or offer him anything, or make any attempt at pleasantries as they had over the course of weeks an entire lifetime of loss ago. It would have been too easy to say the couple's reticence was due to van Daan's presence. Van Daan knew his part well enough not to stamp his feet or huff when it became clear that the meeting was going to be tense. In fact, the Burnses didn't even seem to really acknowledge van Daan: they simply led the men into their family room, sat down stiffly in a synchronized movement, and waited for Martinez to speak.

Despite the obvious strain of his daughter's disappearance, Mr. Burns looked healthy and remarkably vital for his age. He resembled an older Richard Gere in the silver of his hair and the dusting of wrinkles on his face, with a slim nose and defined jaw. His voice was always soft. Mrs. Burns matched her husband in this regard, but that was all: a natural blonde, she had dyed her hair a dark brown, similar to Emily's. The result left her looking washed-out and sickly pale. She must have been a beautiful woman once—her looks now washed away by grief.

"We're working to try to find a possible suspect since we were finally able to recover the body. I must tell you again how sorry I am for your loss. But I have to ask again: Is there *anything* about Emily's disappearance that you've recalled now that we haven't discussed before?" Martinez recited his lines perfectly; beside him, van Daan twitched and fidgeted like a bored child.

"There was nothing unusual about our schedule the week Emily went missing," Mr. Burns said. "I myself was out of town, but Emily texted me after she got out of school that day. She'd had an exam in her earth sciences class and told me she was going to spend the afternoon at the shelter. That was the last time I was in contact with her, and it was completely normal. You know all this. You have my phone records."

"Yes, sir. You were out of town for golf, yes? And Emily texted you again after she left the shelter around seven."

"I believe so. It was her routine."

"Of course." Martinez smiled warmly. "Mrs. Burns, your original statement, you said Emily had a close group of friends that you all knew from a church circle."

"Evelyn, Claire, and Bethany. We've discussed this."

"We did, yes. But is it possible that she might have someone else—anyone else—who might've been close to her?"

"If there were, we would have met them. Emily was always very open with us."

"And there was no boyfriend?" van Daan asked. "I mean, we've talked about this, I know, but—no guy? No 'friend' there in the wings she was talking to?"

"Emily was not allowed to date, Detective." Mrs. Burns sounded far away.

"Yes, ma'am." Martinez had been fiddling with his pen, but he stopped and deposited it in his coat pocket, shooting van Daan a quick glare. "To be perfectly honest, Mr. and Mrs. Burns, we are having a hard time at the station with this. See, the way it looks is, Emily was a model child. And everyone we've interviewed had nothing but praise for her. If there was no boyfriend and there were no problems at home, we only have a few scenarios left. Now, please don't take offense to this." Martinez held his hands palms out and placating. "Were there any substance abuse problems with Emily?"

Mrs. Burns stared. "Don't be ridiculous."

"It's not that ridiculous," van Daan huffed. "Kids take drugs. More often than you'd ever believe. I heard once that—" Martinez coughed and van Daan stopped talking.

"Well, then." Martinez paused to find his footing. "Is it at all possible that there is something else going on here?"

"And *what would that be*, Mr. Martinez?" Mr. Burns asked.

Martinez hesitated, and then reached into his jacket pocket. The compact, which he'd hastily cleaned and then kept on his person at all times, fit neatly in his inner pocket and was warm to the touch as he pulled it out and gently placed on the coffee table in front of the Burnses. Amidst the dirt and crime he'd pulled it from, the simple mirror had been vastly out of place; the mahogany background it rested against now fit together like a key and a lock.

"Do you recognize this?" Martinez asked quietly. Mr. and Mrs. Burns said nothing. "I think you do, and I think you know it used to be your daughter's. We found it buried in the lot not far from her body." A pause, and then: "That may not seem like a big deal, but if it wasn't on her person, then she didn't have it when she died. Someone else put it there." Mrs. Burns flicked her eyes once at Martinez and then averted her gaze.

"Does any of this mean anything to you?" Van Daan leaned forward. "Someone was disturbing the site before we were able to find the body. You say your daughter was perfectly normal, but she was dumped all the way on the other side of town with little to nothing." Martinez leaned in, but van Daan didn't stop. "We are trying to help here. You're trying to tell me that nothing about this seems fishy to you?"

Mr. Burns leaned forward and cocked his head. Martinez leaned back. "We have told you everything about our Emily. You said it yourself: she was a model child." Mr. Burns shook his head. "I will not sit here and allow you to blame us for your own incompetence. As soon as we get the autopsy report, we're taking it straight to a private investigator. I think we've waited on you long enough."

Burnses eyes cut hard to the hallway behind him, and van Daan laughed harshly, but still clapped his hands on his thighs and stood hastily. Martinez cleared his throat. "Mr. Burns, I apologize if you thought we was accusing you or Mrs. Burns of anything untoward about your daughter. Believe me, that's the last thing we think. As for the investigation, we are doing everything we can." Martinez stood. "If you happen to remember anything later on, please let us know."

Mr. Burns stood stiffly beside the sofa but did not extend a hand or wave him on. Mrs. Burns studied the floor. Martinez quickly let himself out in a hurry to catch up with van Daan, who had already shown himself out. The compact, tucked back neatly into Martinez' pocket, had likely never been seen by either parent.

"Those assholes—telling us we're wasting *their* time," van Daan grumbled. "What, did we cut into their tee-time? They only have one kid and they can't admit they didn't know shit about her?"

"That's enough." Martinez unlocked the car. The meeting had gone as well as could be expected, and Martinez had gotten what he really came for anyway. Now he had to consider his other options.

Van Daan had no luck interviewing people near the crime scene and didn't handle the rejection well. Three houses had blatantly refused to answer their doors; it had taken strong counseling to keep him from decorating the block with citations.

The Chief had only wanted to be notified when they made a major breakthrough. Ultimately, contacting the media and setting up a hotline was their last best option. But Martinez was loathe to do it. The response hadn't yet come back from the next town over, but they had promised to be thorough in archiving their records. Still, widening the parameters of their search for answers might turn up the clues they'd been waiting for, and might even win a warmer reception from the Burnses when next they spoke.

For the next week, Martinez didn't have a chance to make the drive back out to Pleasantville. A middle-aged man in a three-piece suit had driven his car headfirst into a tree, and handling that inquiry took up most of his spare time. But his thoughts wandered back to the crime scene at every opportunity, to a cleared area with dead underbrush and small piles of waste. An area cleaved open by the fresh hole they'd dug.

The more he thought about it—and he thought about it more and more with each passing day—the more he was convinced that the site he'd pulled the objects from was the true burial site for his victim. The body they'd pulled from behind the dumpster was just that—a body—and they'd already learned all they could from it. The packing of the dirt spoke of ritual, and the burying of the items suggested guilt. To take the time and effort to bury an object—an object that might have been used every day, that was obviously personal in some way—someone out there in those rolling hills had enough cause and emotion to do it, and it piqued Martinez's curiosity to no end. It was just a feeling, but Martinez was almost certain this behavior hadn't been a one-time act, that if he could only find out who was visiting the site—a name, an address, a description, *something*—he would find his motive. It was too random not to be important.

If van Daan had been allowed to weigh in, he would have called Martinez's ponderings a waste of energy. But that was van Daan all over. Van Daan, who threw fits when witnesses changed their stories or when perps clammed up or when the local burger stand got his order wrong. He was a good cop but a tactless detective, too bullish for the sort of finesse that Martinez strove for.

He kept the compact and studied it often. Although it showed signs of use, there were no traces of dirt or blood anywhere on it, and the label on the back linked it to one of the high-end boutiques near the downtown area. Getting fingerprints wasn't an option, and Martinez bemoaned the wasted opportunity.

A week or so after he'd finished the car crash case, Martinez followed the freeway until he was back in the valley. The sun was beginning to recede along the treetops, and as he passed through, people and cars ebbed away and crept back into the neighborhood crevices. When he got to the clearing, he cut the lights and waited a beat before getting out of the car.

The yellow tape was no different from before, but Martinez still handled it gingerly as he crossed over. He didn't see any new footprints, but as he stilled himself and studied the ground, it hit him: someone had cleared the brush of debris and removed all the trash. Martinez moved further away from the enclosure. The lot itself and the fringes of the area were still matted down with litter and hadn't changed at all, but inside and around the site, the ground had been picked over and groomed meticulously. Martinez eased back over the tape and knelt down. There were no new traces of shoes or hands, but the soil and the grass and the leaves—the feel and smell and sense of someone else was palpable.

Suddenly, Martinez looked up. Across the street from the lot was a small house with a shabby, broken-down porch, but the yard was clean and maintained, and the windows had not been left bare but were covered with curtains. Martinez knew this because the fringe of the front window curtain had been pulled back, and a face was looking directly at him.

Martinez crouched and stared. When he blinked, the face in the window was gone.

He made a point of going back three days later and again two days after that but couldn't find anything else different. One evening, rain fell, froze, and became ice overnight. The next morning brought five wrecks on the freeway and twelve school delays across the city. It was that evening, with the cold biting into the bones of the souls unfortunate enough to be caught cut in it, that he again drifted out to the dark hills, this time parking his car directly in front so as to use his headlights to see.

The original hole where Emily had been dug up had been filled back in and evened out. The second thing was a new set of footprints, preserved in place beside the same bush that held the compact. Picking apart the brush revealed a hair tie with a few gossamer strands clinging to it. He was prepared this time. A set of gloves and a sealed bag helped him pocket and preserve the find.

The pictures he took of the footprint were grainy from the lens of his cellphone. He would have to call forensics and arrange for them to come back out and catalogue it. The ripples and indentations in the dirt were consistent with sneakers, and the feet were small and narrow—youthful. The angle of the prints wasn't a standing position—not completely, not when he was able to see the grooves of knees and the faint imprint of hands. Whoever they were, they had spent time in the dirt too.

The detective's eyes flicked back to the house across the lot. He could not see any movement of the curtain in the dark, but he imagined that the face that had watched him earlier could still see him. He made a point of exaggerating his gestures, just in case.

Martinez took more pictures and thought about contacting the chief as he drove home, but eventually decided not to. The chief had said he only wanted to be informed when a perp had been pulled for questioning, and the sooner they could find that person, the better. He would need something substantial before he could contact him again. As he turned into his drive and parked his car, Martinez thought again of the neatness of the lot. Not far away, another yard had been kept unusually neat as well.

If he came back during the day and approached in a squad car, whoever lived in that neat little house might be better persuaded to talk. Perhaps he would even bring van Daan.

On Monday, she went to school twenty-five minutes late and wasted the first period away in the office while the front secretary called her house and tried to get an excuse out of her mother. The secretary called at least four times before accepting that her story was true: that her mother wasn't home, hadn't taken her to school, and wasn't going to bring a note. The secretary wrote a note herself as the bell for second period rang; she tore it off her notepad and tossed it over the counter toward her before turning away. The young girl took the note carefully and pretended to wait for the secretary to dismiss her until the crowds in the hallway thinned, and then she crept to class.

The florescent lights were blinking in the hallway on the way to her biology class. The school was lukewarm and through the windows along the wall she could see drops of dew still clinging to the wiry tree branches scraping the glass. She walked as slowly as she could. If she didn't come in until the last 15 minutes of class, the teacher might just give her the notes that she needed to study to catch up. That would give her time to figure out what they had done in class last week.

By lunchtime, she'd failed a test in history and gotten caught cheating in algebra. When she got sent back to the office, she didn't even say anything to the secretary playing solitaire on her computer and trying to look busy; she just walked to the chairs on the side and sat down to wait for the end of the school day.

"Ma'am, if you flick that lighter one more time, I'm going to take it away from you."

"Oh, yeah, of course you will. And then I'll slap you with a class-action lawsuit and wear your badge as a trophy, you pig."

"That must be a big word for you, sycophant. Did they teach you that in your night class at the learning annex?"

"Screw you."

Bringing van Daan had been a mistake. Martinez could have guessed how badly things would go as soon as the first door of their search area had been wedged open to reveal an older woman with faded green hair and chipped front teeth, which she bared at them in an impersonation of a rabid dog when they asked to come inside and sit down. The sagging lines in her face contorted in a mask of disdain before they were even able to get her off the porch. Van Daan's face settled into a pinched, focused expression then and there. It was the same expression he wore right before he Tasered someone.

Having wrestled the woman from her grip on the inner door frame, she was now facing them on her narrow stoop like a pit bull, rigid line in her spine and nostrils flaring. The lighter in her hand clicked in time with the staccato of her words, and the clipped rhythm of her speech was a Morse code signaling a meltdown from van Daan if Martinez couldn't get a word in. He cleared his throat to draw attention between the two, and when that didn't work he moved in with his hands out, palms up to appear placating. "Ma'am, we are only here to get some information regarding a homicide case. Your cooperation would be much appreciated."

"That's just you saying you want me to give you a name and an address of another door you can break down. It's all about getting a scapegoat, right? Who's the target this time, gentlemen? What, did someone hit up your donut shop?"

"I am just enthralled with your vocabulary, lady. Looks like you kept all the important teeth, too—for pronunciation, you know."

"*William.*" Martinez placed his hand on van Daan's shoulder and nudged him back. Martinez stepped forward, and the woman slowly shifted her body toward him, though she kept her hard eyes trained on van Daan. "A young girl has been killed, and her body was dumped out here in the valley. Someone has been coming and messing with the crime scene, and we think they know what happened to her. That's why we're here."

The woman gazed into Martinez's face for a long moment. Slowly, she crossed her arms. She held herself rigid, but was soft in the voice as she said, "A lot of people wander this street. It could've been anybody."

"You say that like you already have an idea as to who you might have seen." When she didn't respond he prodded again. "Have you perhaps seen someone wandering around here in the past few days? Someone who sticks out in your mind?"

"There was—someone. A kid, I guess. They had a hoodie on."

"Was this at night?"

"Around two or three in the morning, I guess."

"Could you see what they were doing?"

The woman shifted from side to side. "They climbed over the tape and stood around for a while. I don't know, it was dark. I guess they had something in their pocket, but I don't know for sure."

"When did you say you saw this?"

"Like, last weekend, I guess."

"And you never saw them again?"

"No."

"And you don't know if it was a boy or girl?"

"They have only one light on in the lot, sir, and it doesn't always come on. Okay? I don't have a porch light—you see my porch here, right?—I don't have

shit out here. I didn't even really see her until she was up and walking away."
It took a moment, but Martinez saw the realization of her mistake when it
registered on her face. Immediately, the woman huddled into herself.

Van Daan pushed Martinez aside and hemmed in on her until she forced
him back, her hands in a fighting stance, her lip curled and sneering. "That's a
fine thing—not to say that you knew it was girl until you let it slip. How long
have you been rehearsing this little story?"

"I swear to God, man, if you don't back the hell up—"

"—would waste all of our time today and not even keep your lines straight,
seriously now, I'm calling in to get a warrant—"

"Enough." Martinez forced van Daan back. He turned toward the woman
and lowered his hands. Behind him, van Daan was vibrating with energy. "You
can't make up a story to tell us. You have to tell us the truth. We are asking
for your help here at your house, but if that isn't a good enough incentive to
cooperate, we will take you down to the station and you will be asked to tell us
the truth there."

"Oh, *goddammit.*" The woman turned and spat violently out over the
stoop. "Yes, fine, all right. It was a little girl I've seen once or twice. She walks
up this road to go to school most days in the morning. But even if I did catch
her poking around in that lot, what difference does it make? Just because she
was digging around doesn't make her a killer."

"Even if she wasn't directly involved, she might know who is. What is
this girl's name?"

"It doesn't matter what her name is."

"Where does she live?"

"Under a bridge for all I know."

"Ma'am." Van Daan placed his hand on the left porch post, directly behind
her head. "You have dragged this out long enough. Spit it out or swallow it
down in holding."

The woman sneered at them and shoved past them. She stomped down
the stoop steps toward a battered gray pickup and made to get in. Van Daan
started toward her and grabbed the frame of the door. He would not relinquish
it until Martinez quietly drew him back. The officers watched her leave; at his
side, Martinez could hear van Daan hissing obscenities under his breath. As
the truck pulled out of the driveway, the woman rolled her left window down
and called out to them.

"Her name is Daisy, I think. Something like that. She comes out around
midnight some nights. I told her once or twice to stay out of the lot, but she

wouldn't talk to me. She kept to herself from what I could tell." The woman hesitated then said, "She doesn't seem like a bother; whatever you're doing, do not cause trouble for her." And she revved her engine and drove off.

She got all the way down to the stop sign and undoubtedly would have peeled away from the curb without a second thought, were it not for Martinez, bracing his hands across the hood of her truck and peering into the cracked glass of her windshield. "One more thing, Miss. Where around here can we find this girl?"

The woman glared at the detective and revved the engine of her truck as it trembled in place, but her expression quickly deflated when he stayed calm and steadfast before her. Her eyes shifted away before setting on her hands, braced across the top of her steering wheel. "She comes walking up Alabama Boulevard," the woman muttered. "I don't which house it is, but there are kids that live in the house around that end of the block. Kids her age. You should look there." Martinez nodded once and stepped gamely back to the curb.

The men watched the truck drive away. Once the woman pulled out of sight, Martinez gestured to van Daan to follow him back to their car, and after a beat he did. "Okay, Daisy. Let's hope that that's not a common name around here."

When she got home that night, the house was dark and smelled heavy and stale. She put her bag down on the table and got a glass of water while she looked out the kitchen window. She felt her way through the narrow hallway to the closet and fumbled her way in. There was one blob of a candle left, and she took this and made her way back into the kitchen. She had to go through all the cabinets and three of the drawers before she found a box of matches. When she lit the candle and saw the sparse light, she saw that the candle light made no difference at all. Same old shabby house and even shabbier life. She blew it out and made her way to her bedroom.

She crawled into bed but did not immediately fall asleep. She watched the darkness and listened. She thought about what she would wear for school tomorrow and what she would eat for lunch. She saw the streaks of light from the cars driving past and wondered where the drivers were going.

By the time of the third call, Detective Martinez knew he was being deliberately ignored, and he hesitated before putting his phone down. He thought about who he should try to call next: the Burnses or the chief.

After the last meeting with Emily's parents had gone south, Martinez felt the best thing to do would be to give the couple some time before contacting them again. Van Daan insisted that they'd had enough time already. And after talking to the angry woman from the lot—Carlotta, she'd called herself—Martinez couldn't help but think that if the Burnses knew they were actually closing in on a witness, and that the detectives had some legitimate reason to believe that Emily's body being found in the valley was no accident, they might come around.

But after Martinez had called the Burnses the first time to meet for a follow-up, Mr. Burns informed him with no small amount of indignation that Emily was exactly who they said she was: a clean, responsible girl who was taken advantage of, and "the defamation of her character at the hands of the Sweet Valley Police Department" would not change that. He told Martinez that the family had decided to forego any further involvement with the detectives and "their sham of an investigation" and hired a private investigator of their own.

In addition, Mr. Burns said, the couple had sent a strongly worded email to the chief of police criticizing Martinez and van Daan's attitude toward their work and the Burnses' only child.

"You would do well," Mr. Burns said, gravely, "not to contact us again."

"That's your problem, Leonard," van Daan said after the fact. "There's no room for sentimentality here. This could end up on the news, for chrissakes. If you talk to them again, just count me out."

And here Martinez was, trying to touch base again.

He sighed. The chief hadn't even wanted to hear what the detectives had gathered thus far—he told them to stay the hell away from the couple, that if they needed to be brought in for anything else, he would do it himself.

Martinez picked up his phone and called van Daan. "We need to go to the chief tomorrow," he said. Van Daan began cursing a blue streak and Martinez ignored him. "If I try to talk to anyone else, I want him to know beforehand so I can't be backhanded over it later. See you then." Van Daan said something unprintable, and Martinez ended the call.

Everyone she knew said not to go down Alabama Boulevard unless there was no other alternative, and even then not to waste time and hurry off the street as soon as possible. Alabama Boulevard is where that one kid got clipped by a delivery truck in the middle of the afternoon and the guy didn't stop. It was where the stray dogs wandering up and down the pavement hunting for scraps or a kid to bite, and sometimes they weren't even dogs, but raccoons and rats and the occasional rabid possum. It was where that hooker had been shot down—*no, she wasn't a hooker, she had a boyfriend and they lived over on Fillmore Drive.* Someone else says, *that wasn't her boyfriend,* and on and on it goes. But they always come back to the same point: Don't dawdle on the Alabama block. There's nothing good for you there.

It was hard to avoid the block, though, because that was the quickest route to her house. From school she'd walk straight down Alabama Boulevard, turn left onto Hastings Road, turn right onto Flora Avenue, and then walk straight down the block. Hers was the third house on the right. She cut a straight path all the way down one time in the sixth grade, crossing no streets in between, and a man in a car tossed a half-empty beer bottle out his passenger window. It hit her square in the chest, and she walked the remaining blocks home reeking of skunky beer and what she suspected was piss. From then on, she cut across and across again to make sure she was never in one spot too long.

Walking down Alabama Boulevard was like walking down one of the hallways at her school when the bell rang, people standing on the side leering, people squabbling and shoving, and people drifting aimlessly with no purposes. All kinds of voices echoed off the cracked sidewalk at all hours of the day. Sometimes she wanted to idle on the street long enough to hear their conversations. Every now and again she wanted to feel the presence of something foreign, something *other,* because once she was home there was nothing. There was always a vacuum that enveloped her as soon as she opened the front door of her house. The reverberations of the neighborhood followed her up the mottled lawn, up the three wooden steps to her stoop, and were swallowed whole by the darkness inside.

She had left the candle from the other night on her bedside table. She made her way down the hallway to her room and dropped her bag at the foot of her bed. She stood there in the dark before leaning down and fumbling in a side pocket of her coat for the pack of matches she'd swiped from the corner store. She lit the candle and fostered the fragile flicker of light and watched it dance across the walls of her room. She made a decision and set the candle down so she could toe off her sneakers. She stripped efficiently and dumped her clothes in a wad before kicking them aside. Candle in hand, she made her way to the bathroom at the end of the hall.

Taking baths in the dark was a secret kind of thrill. It was warmth and the slicking slide of water, and she could dip her head below without holding her nose or closing her eyes. Sometimes she would twitch or fidget or sleep, and she was never as grateful for the dark as she was on those nights. Tonight she was content just to float and look for shapes in the shadows.

She was especially grateful to still be able to take a hot bath at the end of every day. Going a month without electricity was hard at first, but she couldn't imagine what the smell of her would be had water been the utility her mother had chosen to cut. Taking baths, washing the dishes, washing her clothes or cooking—simply having water to drink would've been impossible. As soon as the electricity was gone, the girl dipped into the funds she'd squirreled away and bought a box of cheap candles and matches, adjusting everything else along the way. Things like dry food that could be stored outside the refrigerator and didn't need a microwave; dollar-brand detergent in the one scent that didn't sting her nose as she washed her clothes in the bathtub by hand, and the baths she took at night, if only to feel warm before going to sleep.

She hummed to herself as she readied for sleep. By the light of her candle she laid out her clothes for the next day and tried to reason out a plan. She'd been able to stay after school long enough to catch up using the online tutorials for the past two assignments in world history, but biology would be a different story entirely. The class had started a new play without her in English, and her faint inclination toward the school newspaper had evaporated as soon as the new team was announced and her name wasn't on the list. But that was okay because she hadn't really wanted to take on the extra responsibility anyway.

Everything would be fine if she could make it to Thanksgiving break without the school insisting on seeing her mother. As far as she knew, no attempts had been made to contact her, aside from the secretary trying to get a note for her tardiness last week. That secretary never followed through on any of her threats was a consolation. Still, there was the squeaking horde of mice she'd discovered under the kitchen sink. And how could she explain her living situation in a way that wouldn't have the school contacting social services, should they choose to push the issue?

One day at a time; that was the only way. The weekend would come quickly enough, and the school was so busy with their athletics and board meetings that they might not even be aware of her; not little, lonely, homely her, there and gone in an instant. And the icy rainstorms that had been foretold by the weather man hadn't come yet, so there might not be many days left anyway. At the very least, the winds hadn't picked up, so the air was warm enough that even a thin blanket could still suffice.

Martinez went alone to see the chief.

"Our perp has been seen at the site after hours more than once," he began. "There are at least three other people from the neighborhood we can interview, and we have good odds of them all having consistent stories. We have a name and an address."

"For a girl that's just poking around an empty parking lot? Why is this even important?"

"She hasn't just been poking around. She's been leaving things behind."

The Chief leveled a stare at him. "What kind of things?"

Martinez retrieved the compact from his pocket and placed it on the desk within the Chief's reach. The Chief did not reach for it. He looked it over passingly and then his eyes flicked back to Martinez. "You're basing this all off *makeup?*"

"Over the course of some weeks—I would have to guess a month, as least, based on what that lady said—this girl has been coming again and again to this same spot and messing with the stuff that's there. She's been leaving stuff and trying to avoid having people see her—these are visits in the middle of the night at three or four in the morning. The other night when I checked, someone had closed in the holes we'd dug up after retrieving the body. She's tending to the land, and that's—" Martinez cleared his throat. "That's why we think she has a strong connection to the victim. People leave trinkets at and groom a grave. There's a sense of respect there. No one does that for no reason."

"Does the description of this girl match up with anything the parents gave you? Does she go to the same school as our victim?"

"No. But then, that doesn't mean anything. Our victim was found in this girl's neighborhood, and that probably wasn't an accident."

"You're saying this girl is a witness?"

"I'm saying that even if she is just poking around, this girl might know someone, seen something or heard something, and that's what's making her come back every night." Martinez hedged his bets. "We also found a hair tie with some hair on it that we are working now to get a DNA sample on."

"Who do you think it's going to be?"

"Probably the girl. But what if it isn't?"

The Chief sat there and worked his jaw while he watched Martinez . Martinez stared passively back. In his head he was preparing to say that the calls made to Wilton had been useless and wouldn't suddenly become useful later on; that there weren't any other suspects in the system, and it would take a miracle for any of their scant evidence to stand a chance in court; and that it had taken months of working fruitlessly for them to get anywhere on this case, and their biggest break yet had been dug up by a dog.

The Chief looked down at the table and rumbled unhappily from his chest. "When are you going to corner this kid?"

"The address that we got wasn't exact. It was just the neighborhood she's been spotted in."

"So you're going to stalk her until she shows. Essentially."

"Yes. Essentially."

"And what do you plan to tell Channel 5 when somebody calls up and says you're lurking? Hell, what will you tell her parents?"

"The truth. She was ID'd by a member of the community, and we'll be keeping our source anonymous. We got two other people to confirm it. We're not stepping on anybody's rights here."

The Chief leaned back and worked his jaw again as he swiveled his chair to the left. "She might not even talk to you once you reel her in."

"Maybe so."

They waited in silence for a few moments before Martinez let himself out. As he walked out the door he heard the Chief behind him. "What's her name, anyhow?"

"Daisy. She's thirteen."

Martinez had not exactly been truthful when he told the chief he'd gotten a lock on the girl's location, but he hadn't exactly lied, either. He *did* know where she was. There were quite a few blocks in the area Carlotta had indicated was Daisy's house, and after running background checks on the addresses and their occupants, Martinez believed he could find her. When he reported that back to the chief, however, he was told that was not enough. There had to be some precedent for choosing this address and this girl, Hendricks said, and one witness who would never talk to them again wasn't going to be enough. So Martinez and van Daan took a poll of the neighborhood surrounding both Daisy's house and the site where the items had been dumped, and sure enough, they had insights to share. The people in the neighborhood saw her and just assumed she was coming to and from school, sometimes going—"Somewhere, down the block, around the corner, I don't really know, who really cares? She's a kid. And what does it matter, anyway? A body can hang on the corner all day if they want to—you saying you made a law against that too?"

There was one more witness to go, and Martinez knew that if it should go that far, he could be pressed to testify in court. But he was busy during the day, and Martinez would have to catch him when the school day ended.

Martinez left a voicemail, then waited two hours before circling the school and parking in the faculty lot. Three o'clock came and went, and when Martinez came back into the front office there was no one behind the counter. He called again at four; no answer. At a quarter to six, a tall, slim black man in a suit and tie exited the school through the back-gym entrance, got into a cherry-red Cadillac and departed the lot without looking around once. Martinez shifted in gear and calmly revved his car engine.

Principal Stuyvesant lived outside of the valley. His was a neat two-story house with a withered elm tree looming over the lawn and broken shutters on the windows. Martinez followed him over the overpass and through the sprawling neighborhood sedately, absentmindedly noting how he sped through the blocks and didn't yield to other cars. When he got to the house, Detective Martinez parked across the street and was on the lawn by the time the principal got out of his car.

"Is there a reason you tailed me all the way home, sir? Do I need to call the police?"

Martinez flashed his badge and waited while a host of emotions played across Stuyvesant's face. "Detective Leonard Martinez. I called the school a couple times earlier today, and I also called your cell. When you didn't answer, I figured you were just desperate to meet in person."

Principal Stuyvesant laughed humorlessly. "I'm not desperate to meet with the police. But all right, what can I do for you?"

Martinez went into his speech. He needed the name of one of the principals' students, a Daisy something. He didn't know how old she was or what grade she was in, but he did have a general idea of where she lived based on a tip he'd gotten from one of her neighbors. She wasn't in any trouble and there was no need for the school to get involved beyond being helpful; she wasn't a case for CPS and she wasn't being charged with anything.

Principal Stuyvesant barked a laugh, rolled his shoulders, tossed his car keys in the air and snatched them again. He wasn't fooled, and it showed. "What's the name of the student?"

"Daisy."

"What did she do?"

"Nothing. We just need to talk to her."

"And what exactly is it that you want in regards to her?"

"I need what you have on her file," Martinez answered. "Address slips, detention notices, any kind of documentation of her both in-school and out. Basically, everything you can give me."

"And then what?"

"And then nothing. We all move on."

"No, I mean, what happens to the school? Does this have something to do with Sweet Valley? Someone on my staff? She call you to talk about her teachers?"

"No, sir."

The principal turned away and walked onto his porch. He took his time separating his keys and selecting the correct one, and before opening the door he turned back around and faced Martinez. "Call the front desk tomorrow and tell Laura to put you on hold for me. I'll talk to her in the morning so she'll expect you."

Martinez nodded and smiled thinly. "That would be great. Thank you, Mr. Stuyvesant."

Martinez got in his car and went back the way he'd come, going back far enough that he could get onto the highway, headed back to the precinct. Only then did it occur to him that for all the time he had spent looking for this girl, he had no idea what she looked like.

Her mother said she would call Monday night. Monday night her mother would call. Don't dawdle when you get out of school and don't spend too much time on the block but do go to school and walk home; don't take any rides from nobody. And she did just that, at least in part; she darted out of her house light-footed and sprightly in the morning, practically flying on the way home in the afternoon. It was the first call she'd gotten from her mother in three weeks.

When she got home, hopeful and anxious, she cleaned the house like she was preparing for her mother's arrival rather than just her call. Her mother had given her a cellphone without knowing that she'd had one before. That one was now gone; her new one required a prepaid card for minutes and texts every 60 days. She was able to stretch the minutes for their entire duration simply because no one ever contacted her aside from her mother.

That was not to say they weren't used to the fullest. She'd used it to set up a study session with a classmate in history last semester, and they met once at the girl's house. When the time came for her to arrange a second meeting at her own house, she ignored her classmate's calls; ignored what it cost her phone account to save the ugly voicemails that came after. Eventually, she accepted a failing grade for her portion of the project, and the other girl spread a rumor about her in the weeks that followed. She called gas stations to confirm their hours until she had their schedules memorized. Once, she'd tried to call and order a pizza, but hid in the hallway when the delivery man came, realizing too late that she didn't have enough change. The newness of her mother's absence had long worn off by then.

Her mother had given her the cell phone and sent her phone cards almost always on strict schedule. She sent money in grungy envelopes so that Daisy could buy groceries, and when a bill came she would pay what she could. They had stopped talking about when she would come home. The last time they'd spoken she had promised a week, maybe two, before the doctor would get back to her with a new consultation. At the very least, her mother would call her that night.

She always hesitated to do so, but tonight she was going to ask for some extra money. There was enough food to last her another week, but she had burned through her last candle over the weekend, and getting through the nights at the house without them was a shadow shy of unbearable. Going too many days without some source of light would put her too far behind on her homework, and that would put her in her teachers' crosshairs. They would try to call home again, and when there was no connected line to reach, they would call her back into the office and try to wrangle the information out of her again—then straight to her house they would go, leading her along, right to the last clustered shards of her lives. *You don't want that, do you, Daisy?*

Hopefully when her mother called she wouldn't want to talk about Mrs. Flanders, like she had last time. That was starting to be a hard thing to beg off. "Mrs. Flanders is in a better place now, Ma. Mrs. Flanders went peaceful as could be. What? Mom, I told you: I really am okay." No need to reminisce about an old hag gone and dusted. "Can we talk about something else?"

When she got to her house, the cat that she used to feed was prowling skittishly across the lawn. The dead grass crackled under her feet. She ignored the creature's plaintive yowls as she made to unlock her door. The dark was warm and damp, adulterated by the sunlight sifting in through half-closed curtains. She went to the kitchen for a glass of water and wandered slowly into her room to rest. She laid down and contented herself to wait. The phone rested on the pillow beside her head.

She was a dirty little thing. That was his first thought.

The face in the picture wasn't dirty, but there was a certain sheen to that skin that suggested poor hygiene. Her chin and forehead were oily. Her sandy blonde hair was a limp shroud, and this only confirmed his suspicions that this girl's life had been marked with bouts of homelessness.

It would've been better if he'd been able to see her teeth. Her mouth was closed and unsmiling, but her lips were thin and faintly pink, the same color that dusted her cheeks. Her eyes were a pale blue. He noted with some interest that her left eyebrow was slit in half by a jagged shining line; the wound had not healed easily. Not a pretty girl, not at all, Martinez mused. A frail little thing with a lukewarm glare, daring someone to say something.

Martinez had followed Principal Stuyvesant's instructions and as a result, he had gotten the file he wanted; before delving into it, he called back to ask for a photo, and the principal warned that the only one they had was from the previous school year. Daisy hadn't brought the money for a new photo on picture day. "Honestly, if this is the same girl I'm thinking of, she showed up to school in flip flops the day we got that huge snowstorm. Kid ain't got no kind of sense."

Daisy Young had not shown up for her first class on that day and wasn't waiting in the office to get a late pass. That meant they couldn't pick her up at the school, and the principal was unabashedly relieved as he asked again if Martinez need anything else. "Because if she hasn't shown up by second period, she won't be coming in today, you know? And who knows if she'll show up tomorrow. And I'm willing to bet you want to get a move on this—am I right?"

So Martinez emailed the Chief, texted van Daan, and got in his car. As he merged onto the interstate, he listened to the weather reports on the radio. The jockey promised no less than five inches of rain, and Martinez' imagination flared up like skin over a bruise. He drove over the pass and took on speed after a sharp left turn.

The site hadn't been checked since Martinez retrieved the hair the weeks before. There was no point. The yellow tape waved like decrepit streamers in the breeze. Patches of weeds clung to the earth, brittle and dry. Martinez stepped lightly through the lot with singular focus.

He stopped when he found a plastic bag that lay half-buried in the dirt.

The bag had probably been completely buried at some point, but there were no discernible marks in the soil to indicate animal interference. Martinez wrapped his hands around the mound and dug in, expecting the bag to be empty. When it didn't give, he dug his fingers in further and pulled. The wrapping disintegrated in his grip, and the bundle was tattered and damp. He shook off the dirt and peeled off the plastic.

Martinez cursed under his breath. There was no telling how much more he could've accomplished if he'd just come out and checked sooner. He dropped down and dug down with both hands, looking for anything else he might've missed.

When he got back to the car he put his key in the ignition and called the Chief. The Chief didn't answer, and he left a voicemail. He called van Daan as he headed back down the street. Waiting at a stoplight, he called the station to have a conference room set up. He would call the lab later.

Van Daan was doing that thing where he wanted to say something rude and for whatever reason was holding himself back. It started as him hunching his shoulders and shoving his hands into his armpits; after he squared his feet and tucked his chin into his chest, he resembled a toddler bearing the brunt of a lecture. Such a behavior was rare for his partner, so Martinez was content to wait and let the burly redhead get his thoughts together while they sat at their desks. Filling out inventory and requisition forms was tedious, mundane work. Van Daan would tell him sooner or later, if only to give himself something else to focus on.

"Almost done over there?" Martinez asked mildly.

Van Daan looked at him blankly. Then he said, "You think she was abused?"

"The girl? Daisy?"

"Yes."

Martinez nodded once. "But I don't think it really matters."

"What do you mean? Of course it matters." He paused. "Doesn't it?"

"Poverty and drug use are par for the course in the valley. Nine times out of ten, the welfare checks and disturbance calls are in those blocks." Martinez was neutral and matter-of-fact. "Given the stats, you would have to assume there's abuse going on. Neglect, beatings. The sexual stuff and whatnot." He shrugged. "I think it's a safe bet that there's some kind of home turmoil. I just don't think it's relevant to the crime itself."

"There doesn't seem to be any relevance of any kind to any of it at all." Van Daan shook his head and fanned his hands out across his paperwork. "I mean, they have nothing in common, these two girls—nothing. We have no prints, no forensics. They don't have anything that ties them together. Just—" Van Daan shook his head again. "But if she was abused, your girl, that makes more sense to me. Kids can get into some weird shit, especially if they have problems. What if she just stole it off the corpse, huh?"

"That would still mean she knew where the body was. Maybe she saw who buried it. In that case, we really need to talk to her. She could be a witness." At van Daan's expression, Martinez sighed. "I have a strong feeling about this. Okay? Did you even look at the compact closely?" Van Daan made a mild noise of disgust. Martinez schooled his expression and explained, "The thing came from a boutique across town. *Bella La Vie* or some nonsense. Way out of the valley. What teenage girl in the hills has the cash to waste on something like that? Little thing was thirty bucks. She may have stolen if off the body, but even if she did, I still want to talk to her. Who else do we have to talk to at this point?" Martinez turned back to his forms.

A moment later, van Daan sighed loudly. "Ah, well. If that's it, then." He resumed his paperwork too.

Her mother wouldn't give her any money. She said she didn't have any extra cash to send; something about there being a higher balance due this month than last month, "and besides, you still have food, don't you sweetie? Aren't you still staying with Mrs. Flanders? Honestly, if you aren't, you should be. It's not safe to be out alone, and I know you aren't comfortable there at the house, that's what you said, but…" The safest option—her mother always found a way back to that. What did that even mean at this point? Safety was as relative as the weather. "I'm just thinking of you, honey."

She mumbled monosyllabic answers for fifteen minutes and tore threads off her bedspread as she listened to her mother rattle on about a squirrel she'd seen in her front yard that morning. She backed out of saying goodbye and hung up before her mother could finish talking. Closing her eyes, she breathed deep and counted to ten in her head.

The phone flew out of her hand and ricocheted off the wall, landing in pieces.

It was only just darkening outside when she finally left the house. Quick steps brought her up through the block to the corner, and she jogged across the crosswalk even with no cars in sight. She was going to take Alabama Boulevard and get there quickly. In and out, because the corner store closed at nine, but she had to make a stop first.

No lights were on, and the car was absent from the drive. That was a positive sign. As she let herself in through the rickety front gate, she reached out to the mailbox, once painted baby blue, and tried again to straighten it in its post in the ground. When she couldn't, she sighed and tucked the mail back inside. The rosebush that had seemed so lively a year before had curled in on itself and died. She fished her key out of her jacket pocket and pressed in to the front door.

The lock hadn't been changed. She ducked inside; the heat and cloying smells made her cough still, and emotion, ugly and all-consuming, surged in her, making her tremble, making her want to cry and run back. She made her way slowly to the staircase on her left. She was careful on the broken sixth step, and upon reaching the top she veered off to the right.

The bed had been shoved away and the dresser was gone. She made her way to the closet, stumbling over shapeless rubble as she went. The bottom of it was littered with papers and dust and assorted nothings, which she sifted through to find the hidden latch. She jimmied it loose, felt around, grabbed what she needed. She reached out for the door frame behind her to steady herself, and then she reared up and turned to go.

As she turned, a hand wrapped around her throat and squeezed. "What the hell is this?" growled a voice, but she had no air left to scream.

"Are you sure this isn't the same house that was condemned?"

"No. We would've been able to pull the paperwork if it had."

"Well, I'm not sure it shouldn't be. This place is a dump."

"Yes," Martinez sighed. "It is."

Admittedly, the house was a little decrepit. Its character suggested a valiant struggle against the ravages of time and poverty, but, as Martinez pointed out, the house looked no different than any of the others on the block. Compared to some Martinez had driven past that day, it might've even been an improvement.

"Well, she's not here. When did we first check in?"

"Around three or four."

"And what time is it now?"

"It's, uh—hold on—almost ten."

"So we been out here for at least six hours? Here in the ghetto, pounding the pavement? Beating the block? Hounding the hustlers?"

Martinez made a huffing sound that wasn't quite a laugh. "Yes."

"And we still ain't turned this girl out, right?"

"No."

"So what does that tell you?"

For a second Martinez thought he saw a sliver of a face peeking out from behind the blanket covering the window on the side of the house. Then he blinked, and the face was gone. "No. Tell me."

"Well, I don't know about you, but two things have become abundantly clear to me." Van Daan was tapping at the wheel listlessly.

"Enlighten me."

"It's simple: You either need to give up on this girl, or you need to change your approach."

Martinez rolled his eyes and shifted in his seat. "How should I do that, Daan?"

"Do what?" Van Daan opened his car door, leaned over, and spit into the pavement. "Change your approach?"

Martinez nodded.

"You only got this one address and you only got a few stories. Stories from people who will say just about anything. But word of mouth don't always mean shit. Why don't you find out for yourself? Go inside."

No one was visible on the block. Martinez turned to van Daan. "What?"

"The door isn't locked, man. No reason it would be. Go inside."

Martinez looked at him. "We don't have a warrant."

"Go inside."

"If anyone finds out, we won't be able to question her."

"Go inside."

"The report will be wasted, even if we find anything they'll never accept it."

"Man, go the hell *inside*. There's no one in that house. And even if there is, so what? You think the people that live here know their rights? What do you think the Chief is going to say to you if you can't get this girl to the precinct? You think he'll let it slide that you already spent all this time for nothing? Man, just—" Van Daan grabbed his shoulder and jostled him. Martinez moved with the motion woodenly. "Go in real quick and look for something we can use. I'll keep watch."

Martinez bit down on the inside of his cheek and ignored van Daan's glare. His jaw clenched. He got out of the car and closed the door quietly.

He crossed the street without looking back.

The door *was* unlocked. The lights were off, and the closest light switch along the wall produced nothing. He had a flashlight, but it was too small to be of much use, and he was blinded by his ignorance as he shone it around the furniture that huddled around him. He felt helpless and unwelcome. From what he could tell, there was a couch, a coffee table, and no television. There were no pictures, save for a portrait hanging on the wall towards the hallway. Martinez leaned in with his flashlight. It was a picture of a farmhouse.

The kitchen and living room were connected in an open space. The kitchen was nearly empty. On a whim, Martinez opened the refrigerator. The light inside wouldn't turn on and the stench of rotten food told him it hadn't been opened in weeks. There was a fine film of dust on the counters he ran his fingers across. Backing out slowly, he moved further into the maw of darkness and found his way down the hallway.

He found the bathroom next, but bypassed it after his flashlight caught a door with a Maroon 5 poster. He was in the girl's room and was just reaching out when his cell phone rang. The noise was so loud that he jumped and cursed, dropping his phone and scrambling to answer before the call ended.

It was van Daan, telling him he needed to come outside immediately. Martinez called him an asshole and hung up before opening the door.

Her bed was a bundle of blankets and wrinkled clothes. Desperate to resist his anxiety, Martinez cast cursory glances over everything he could see; something he could stuff in his pockets and leave with. In the next moment van Daan was calling again, and Martinez barked into the tiny speaker. "What is it? Is there someone out there?"

"We got a call from Ferguson." Van Daan's voice was strangely harried. "His patrol's out here tonight and he got a pair in for assault and a suspected break-in."

Martinez palmed his face and shifted the flashlight to the other hand. "Damn it, Will, what does that matter?"

"The pair were brought in together, but they aren't *together*. One of 'em's a fifty-year-old sex offender. Says he was asleep when a little girl broke into his house and tried to steal some stuff that belongs to his late mother. Girl, on the other hand, is saying he put his hands on her—put his hands around her neck and held her down. She's crying rape."

"So *what*, Daan? Isn't Ferguson out on patrol tonight? Why can't he take it?" Was that an owl outside the window? He couldn't tell, because like all the other windows there was a thin blanket covering the frame. He stared at the material before he realized the blanket was actually a bed sheet. Martinez moved closer, slow and distracted by the thought of another bed sheet, bagged up in the station. Another bed sheet, baby blue with little yellow stars, stained with dirt and grease and hair that they could not remove.

Martinez blinked slowly. He was watching his fist tighten around the material covering the window and couldn't hear van Daan still talking in his ear, not at first.

"Did you hear me, Marty? We have to go *now*, man, the Chief will be calling us back soon. Ferguson just dropped them off at the station. We can't take too long to get there."

When he finally got back to the squad car, Detective Martinez felt numb. They needed the girl. *They needed the girl.* He kept hearing the words in his head over and over again that he didn't notice van Daan had stepped out of the car and walked around to him. He was shoving something in his face.

"Ferguson just texted us pictures of our new case. I kind of recognize the dude, but have you ever seen the girl?"

Martinez grabbed at the cell phone blindly and squinted at it. His eyes widened, and he paused long enough to say, "Yes," before he was scrambling to get in the car. Had there not been a stop sign at the end of the block, he would've left van Daan at the curb of the street.

For the duration of the ride, Martinez didn't speak. Van Daan adapted to the atmosphere and didn't attempt small talk.

Going to case the house had been a bust, but it didn't matter: *they had the girl.* Sullen, dirty, and now discovered. She was waiting at the station, and the sensation Martinez had been chasing the entire time was washing over him in steady waves. This was the end of his hunt, and now the case would be closed. He had the feeling of closure now, and his instincts were never wrong.

When he pulled into the station, van Daan cleared his throat. "We will only get one crack at this," he said quietly. Soberly. "I hope your theory pans out."

Martinez smiled, clear and triumphant.

THE WAITING ROOM

SHE'D SEEN ROOMS LIKE THIS on cop shows. All the pieces were there: the hard furniture, the bare walls, and the buzzing noise from the white overhead light. The silence was a little unnerving, but she resolved herself not to speak. *Don't say anything. Don't say anything, and eventually they have to let you go.* That's the way it always worked.

It was the inscrutable silence that made every little sound roar in her ears. The scratchy whispers of her sweater when she shifted; the scraping, scuffling sound of her feet dragging on the grooves in the carpet; police sirens still screaming in her head. There were murmurs seeping through the walls, growing steadily louder.

The door opened slowly behind her.

Two men came in. They were the cops from before, but they looked more natural in the confines of their building than they had on the street. She hadn't gotten a chance to get a good look at them before when they had appeared out of shadows and seized her with arms spidery and elongated; before it was shouts and boots kicking at the floor near her head. Rough hands grasped her and dragged her up as another set grappled with Patrick. He kicked and flailed something awful; someone must have struck him to subdue him, because she heard him suck in a breath and exhale in a huff, crying in earnest; the hands on her gentled long enough to cover her up and guide her into the squad car.

Somewhere close by, Patrick was saying over and over again that she broke into his house, she broke into his property. "Broke into my damn house and attacked me, troubled little shit."

Somewhere else a grim voice was chuckling and telling Patrick he was a lying sack of shit. "Yeah, a short little thing like her was knocking you out with what—eyeliner and an empty tin box? How does ripping her shirt open help you defend yourself?"

She was aware that other cops in uniform came and swarmed the house, filled it with noise and flashing lights. She laid down in the backseat as they took her away and watched the night sky flashing through the tinted glass. Hands dragged her up and out, sent her stumbling into the station. A brown-bricked, nondescript building with no other cars and no Patrick; the corridors were a maze until they deposited her into the holding room and left her, disheveled, feeling small and numb.

Now she looked at the officers standing before her and tried to communicate her disdain through her eyes. One of the men was white with shiny red hair and a round, squashed face. He was portly but solid, boxed into frame by a brown blazer. He may have had all the comforts of a good life, but he was bitter faced and didn't appear to enjoy it.

The other one didn't look so mean. He was Hispanic, with dark skin and shiny black hair. His forehead was finely creased, and his cheeks bristled with stubble. Thin-lipped and slighter than his counterpart, he looked to be the more delicate of the two.

The men seated themselves at the table and faced her passively for a few moments. "Have you had enough time to get yourself together?" the white cop asked; he was the one who drove her to the station. She'd listened to him mutter unintelligible things under his breath through three stoplights before he finally cut himself off with a curse. She ignored his question and angled her body away.

"Let's get introductions out of the way. I am Detective Martinez, and this is my partner, Detective van Daan." The other cop had a tint of accent in his voice, but his tone was perfectly even. "We want to go over some basics and let you know that as a minor, we cannot ask you any questions about what happened with Mr. Flanders without a parent or legal guardian to consent. So, who do you live with?"

She answered without looking up. "My mom."

"We've already been to your house and there was no car parked outside. It appears that no one's been there all day. Where does your mother work?"

"My mother doesn't— She works out of town."

The redheaded cop was staring hard at her. "Your mother doesn't work, or your mother works out of town?"

"My mother works out of town," she answered quickly. "She's a nurse."

"Which hospital does she work at?"

"Riverbend."

"Riverbend Oncology? Over there in Halbart?"

She nodded. There was a spot that itched in the middle of her back, and she twitched miserably.

"What's your mom's name?"

"Allison."

"All right, then. That's great. We'll be happy to meet Mrs. Young, just as soon as she gets up here." White Cop had a voice that couldn't be quieted. That's what it seemed like as he leaned in and his voice barged in and out of her eardrums. "Now, we're coming up on the wee hours of the morning. You know her cell number? Is she on shift right now?"

The itch was an ache now; it lodged in the center of her back and stretched across her wrists; it was throbbing in her chest and thudding in her ears. "My mom isn't—she won't—that's not—it's just—"

"Hey. Look at me." The Hispanic cop was talking now. His voice was low, and she fought the urge to lash out. "Look at me. Tell the truth. Your mother isn't at work. Where is she?"

If you didn't talk, eventually they had to let you go. That was the way it worked. "My mom isn't nowhere. And you said if she isn't here you can't talk to me."

She snuck a look at them from behind her hair. The Hispanic cop looked thoughtful, and the white cop looked mutinous. He moved so suddenly and was so loud as he kicked back his chair that he startled her; she cowered as he stalked past her and left the room. He made thumping, stomping noises all the way down the hall.

The Hispanic cop was still watching her. He folded his hands delicately on the table and held himself rigidly still. When he spoke, he directed his words to his fingers. "Your mother isn't at work right now, and we know it. You're afraid to call her, and that's fine. But what happened tonight isn't going to go away, and your mother deserves to know about it so she can help you. So we can help you too. The law says we can't begin that process if she's not here. And what's more"—he still didn't look at her—"is that we can't release you until she gets here." He sat there quietly, and she did the same. Eventually, he got up from the table and exited the room. Meeting that douchebag partner of his elsewhere, probably. He could get away with that. He and his partner could get up and leave at any time, leave the whole damn building if they desired, go wherever they wanted, but she couldn't call her mother and she couldn't leave.

And borne out of the silence came the sudden strangled sounds of shouts coming from some corner, and it sounded a lot like Patrick—

She opened her mouth wide in a snarl and meant to scream too, but all that came out was air.

Allison Young wasn't Allison Young. She was Allison Sims, and, lo and behold, she didn't work at Riverbend Oncology.

It became glaringly obvious that Sims hadn't had a job for at least the past six months, but it was probably longer than that. What was less obvious was how she had been providing for her daughter and keeping up with their bills during that time. Van Daan speculated that perhaps a drugs or prostitution had come into play, but Sims had no arrests or charges on her record, save a four-month stint she'd served in the county jail for unpaid tickets and a suspended license. That had been a few years ago, and there had been no additions to her file since.

"So what?" the chief remarked. "She just hasn't been caught yet. Or she put out a fake name so it wouldn't be tied to her real one."

"That doesn't necessarily matter at this point," Martinez said. The Chief was flipping through the paperwork with a disdainful flick of his wrist with every page. Something in the paperwork made him *harrumph* in the back of his throat as he looked up.

"Criminal or not, where the hell *is* this woman? She hasn't come to the station, hasn't stopped back at the house where we picked up the girl. Have we even made contact?"

Put under pressure, Daisy had finally cracked and given the detectives her mother's cell number, but they called multiple times with no response. At least four hours had passed since she had been brought in. Patrick had already been charged, booked and processed. The department had never waited so long to have a parent come claim a child.

"We keep trying the cell and no one answers. She keeps insisting that's the only number we can use to reach her, and that she's just not answering because she's at work."

"Maybe she doesn't know." When the others shot incredulous looks at him, Martinez shrugged and looked down at his hands. "She could just be repeating what she's told. Clearly, she and her mother don't have contact on the regular."

"That's bullshit. It's all bullshit." From the doorway van Daan was smacking his gums and rolling his eyes. His agitation was ridiculous. "We got so much riding on the little tart, but we got *nothing* to leverage against her, and we can't even *talk* to her."

"Did the lab finish the tests on the stuff we brought in?"

"Only on the scrunchie. They tested the hairs to Emily and it wasn't a match. They want to get a sample on the girl, but we can't without parent's consent." The Chief flipped the folder closed and shoved it away from him. "Bottom line, we can't do anything without the mother or a guardian. Can't get fingerprints, can't get a DNA sample, can't take a statement. Someone needs to rustle up."

"Well, what about her father? Do we know anything about him?"

"Name on the certificate is Daniel Young."

Martinez cracked his knuckles and sighed, scratching the back of his head absently. "He went down for first degree murder in 2001. Daisy was born the next year."

"Shit," the Chief groaned. "Well, what else do we have?"

The group was quiet. Martinez was still scratching his head and studying his shoes. "We need to get her to talk about Mrs. Flanders."

"Mrs. Flanders? Why?"

"Well, Patrick said she was breaking in when he…intercepted her, and that's when we came in. But she had a key to the house with her initials on it. How can you break in to a house when you have a key? And the stuff she was trying to lift from the house was in Mrs. Flanders's old bedroom, in the closet, under a loose floorboard. That's awfully specific for a random break-in."

"Was Mrs. Flanders Daisy's neighbor?" asked the Chief.

"Give or take a couple blocks."

"Mrs. Flanders died in the fall," van Daan said. "And wasn't she, like, ninety? Died of natural causes?"

"The report says she died in hospice care." Martinez addressed the Chief. "Patrick signed away her power of attorney after she fell and broke her left hip. We talked to the EMTs that filed the report. Patrick showed up to sign the paperwork, and that was it. Tried to leave with his mother's purse. Hospital security ended up having to escort him off."

"He's a sack of shit. But that was still months ago." The Chief was staring at a fixed point on the wall. "Even if she was welcome in the house while the old lady was alive, why go back now that Mrs. Flanders is dead?"

Martinez spread his hands in front of him. "I don't know. Daisy would know. We need to get her to talk."

The detectives did not reenter the room to tell Daisy that they could not locate or contact her mother—and had no real hopes of changing that during the night. They brought her a bottle of water, a sandwich, and some chips from the vending machine in the lounge and exited quickly. On the camera they could watch her rocking back and forth and bobbing her head, perhaps talking to herself at an angle they couldn't see.

"In the meantime," the Chief muttered, "get Flanders in a room and find out what he can give us. Might have some dirt on the girl."

"That girl is a waste, man. She ain't nothing but trouble. You know how long I been knowing this girl? Since she was a kid, man, a real little kid. And now she saying I raped her? That's crazy, man. I don't have nothing else to say about that."

The processing staff told Martinez that Mr. Flanders had been belligerent, but not combative while they'd been handling him. He wasn't violent or suicidal, hadn't come in with a weapon or any substances on him. He had come in intoxicated but sobered up quickly enough to be brought back into an interrogation room for questioning. Still in the jumpsuit they'd furnished, army green in stark contrast against the whitewashed walls, the stench of alcohol had been sapped from him; his attitude, however, had not.

"I don't think I need to tell you how ridiculous that sounds," Martinez began. "Yes, she might have broken in to your late mother's house, but—"

"My house."

"Excuse me?"

"You keep calling it my mother's house, but it's my house now. That house belongs to me."

"Did your mother will it to you? Was the mortgage transferred over to you?"

"My mother never made no will, and I don't know nothing about no mortgage. My mother wasn't right by the end there."

Had van Daan been allowed to be a part of the interrogation, he would have leaned over the narrow table and snarled *Then it isn't really your house, now is it?* But Martinez merely leaned back, flicked his wrist, waited until he made direct eye contact with Flanders. "You've already been charged and booked for your part in this. Now we need to move on from that and figure out what she was doing in the house in the first place."

"The hell should I know, man?" Flanders flung his arms wide. "That girl is trouble."

"Is there any particular reason why you keep saying that? Is there anything specific she's ever even done to you?"

"I had to put my mom in that home because that little bitch pushed her. Knocked her down the stairs and just left her." Flanders's voice trembled like a child on the verge of a tantrum. "Ma started to die the first day there, man. She was killed, man, killed like an animal."

There was a faint thumping noise from outside the room that Martinez was almost certain was van Daan. Flanders was looking around the room, his eyes wide and crazed as they bounced from spot to spot. Flanders's file had clearly hinted that he had a mental disability and had dabbled with drugs in his youth, but it was impossible to tell where one ended and the other began. At fifty-four years old, he had never held down a job longer than a year.

"What do you mean by that, Patrick? Why are you saying that?"

"Because she killed my mom, man. My mom helped her out when she didn't have nowhere to go, and she pushed her down the stairs. She killed her." Flanders moaned low in his throat. In a slow-motion convulsion he curled into himself and shivered violently. "She killed my mom. She killed my mom. That was the only person I ever had, and now she's gone." His cuffed hands cradled his head; he whined like a wounded animal. Martinez smelled the panic as pungent as sweat from where he sat.

In the end, they hauled Flanders away to a holding cell for the night. Questioning him further would be useless; his face was still glistening with tears as he stumbled down the corridor. "When this is all over, they'll get Dr. Fitz in to see him, see what meds they can put him on. It's just as well. He was bound to lose that house anyway," the Chief said.

"Good riddance," van Daan huffed, and Martinez said nothing. He was still listening to Flanders's hoarse sobbing, waiting in the foyer for the pickup van, when outside his office the Chief's bark cut through Martinez's thoughts.

"The mother just called. She's coming out of Halbart, should be here in about an hour. She gave us the go-ahead on Daisy. Get in there, now."

"How did you want to do it?"

They were walking down the hall together, Martinez with his notepad and a pen, van Daan with his hands hanging down by his sides. The girl lay in the waiting room, and Martinez was feeling calm. Serene, even. These were the moments he worked for, and in his self-assurance he felt guaranteed to get at least some of the answers he wanted. They only had to talk to her first.

He glanced at van Daan. "What do you mean?"

"Who do you want to ask the questions? Me or you? I mean, what's our strategy?"

Martinez blinked, and stopped in front of the door. "Strategy?"

"She is not going to want to talk to us willingly. You ask a question, she'll try to give you a sob story about how she didn't see anything, didn't do anything, blah blah blah. At least if she tries that with me, I'll go on and on until she has to give me something. Then you go in to finish her off."

"Finish her off? Is she some prison vet robbing the park in between parole breaks?" Martinez's tone was incredulous. "This is a kid, D. A kid who's messed up, but a kid nonetheless. We're going to tell her what we know and ask her what we want to know." Martinez shook his head and sighed. "You should never have children, my friend. You can't even talk to them correctly."

"Well, that's all fine, but I think you're forgetting something: If she is who you think she is, the last thing she's going to do is admit point blank everything she might be involved in. What kid is that dumb? 'Oh, yes sir, I stole the merch! Oh, and by the way, I've been sneaking out and burying the shit I stole on the side.' No kid that does that will ever tell *you* that."

"How do you know? How many kids from broken homes do you ever sit down and listen to?" Martinez was confident. "All we can do is ask."

Van Daan scowled. "Fine. Whatever. You just wait until she's spouting off at the mouth and see how charitable you're feeling then. She is going to lie to you and spin you in circles until the mother comes to drag her out."

"The thing is, D, we know that, but she doesn't know that. Get what I'm saying?" Martinez reached for the doorknob. "If we need to, we can drag this out too. Eventually, we'll all get what we want without the drama." He opened the door and ducked inside.

Van Daan huffed but followed his partner.

Her mother gave them permission to talk to Daisy and ask any questions they wanted. They'd kept her secured in the meantime. Now that her mother had said yes, they said, she had to tell them everything or she would not be released into her mother's custody. The vicious white one—van what?—told her this with a shark's smile. She was halved by a desire to claw his eyes out and cry until all the hysteria drained from her.

Mrs. Flanders had agreed to watch over Daisy while her mother was out of town. The arrangement had begun in May, right after school let out. Fact was, Ms. Sims was going to be gone for weeks at a time to work, and Patrick had accused the Filipino physical therapist of stealing the last vestiges of the family wealth a piece at a time.

Despite this and his mother's ever-increasing frailty, Patrick couldn't be convinced that staying home with his mother was a worthwhile use of his time, and Mrs. Flanders had a preternatural fear of leaving the home, as the only thing more frightening than the shadows *inside* her house was the darkness *outside*. Mrs. Flanders clearly needed someone to keep the house livable, buy cheap groceries, and help her maintain some semblance of independence. Ms. Sims has assured her that Daisy was quiet, mature, and responsible. This was a girl who could be trusted with the care of a woman seeking to maintain her dignity while still living at home.

Their deal struck, Ms. Young was gone by the first week of June, and things seemed to work out—for a while. Mrs. Flanders fell in early September, rendering her weaker still, and the arrangement, which was only supposed to last for the duration of the summer, extended into the first few months of the school year. Then things changed abruptly. Within a week of her fall, Mrs. Flanders was moved into hospice care, and she passed away in November.

Most of the information the detectives had gleaned came from half-hearted grunts from Patrick and whispered admissions from Ms. Sims. When she arrived at the station, they didn't bother with greetings; they were already back in the interrogation room with Daisy, nudging her toward a confession.

"I didn't kill Mrs. Flanders, and I didn't break her hip. Patrick is lying."

"Why would he do that?" Detective Martinez asked. "He seems pretty convinced that you pushed her down the stairs. He claimed you tried to kill her."

"How would he know? His mother kicked him out of the house all the time, he was almost never around. He's violent—did he tell you that? He talks to himself, punches walls—he killed a stray dog once. Dude is batshit crazy."

"Language," the other cop said. The Mexican one—Martinez. One of the girls' assistant coaches was a Mr. Martinez, and Daisy noticed now that they had the same haircut. This Martinez was writing notes in a messy scrawl on a pad. She wanted to ask to read the book report he was writing on her, but the other cop was making grumbling noises and taking up all the air in the space between them.

"You say you never hurt Mrs. Flanders and that her son is a liar. Did he ever show any aggressive behavior to his mother before, like a specific incident? Or to you, before tonight?"

Daisy's expression closed off, and she averted her eyes.

"Fine. That practically *screams* yes to me. What about this—why go back to the house if you knew Mrs. Flanders was dead and Patrick was there?" van Daan asked.

She stared at the wall behind their shoulders and stayed silent.

"We can sit here as long as it takes, you know. You're not doing anyone any favors by not saying anything. Especially not you."

There was a sharp rap against the door. The ginger cop kicked away from the table with a huff and darted outside.

The Hispanic cop continued to write on his pad throughout the exchange, and Daisy was sure he knew she was watching him. "What are you writing?"

"You got into the house with a key that had your initials on it," he said. "When did Mrs. Flanders have a key made for you?"

"At the beginning of the summer. What are you writing?"

"What were you trying to take from her old bedroom?"

"Who said I was trying to take anything?" The more she studied his face, the more she noticed the faint lines that were embedded in the contours of his forehead and cheeks. They were light enough to be creases in a canvas. "Did Patrick say that?"

"You didn't set the floorboard all the way back. And the tin was empty. What was in it?"

"Where's my mom?" Her palms were sweating, and her head was thrumming. They knew; knew about the tin and the floorboard, and Patrick was an absolute waste. "You told me my mom was on her way. Where is she now?"

"You're going to have to start answering my questions." Martinez put his pen down and nudged the pad aside. "You broke into a woman's home, and I don't think you've considered the legal consequences that come with that. As a minor, you'll be charged and tried in juvenile court, and from there—who knows?" He swept a hand out across the table as though gesturing across an abyss. "It's your first offense. You'll probably get counseling, community service, probation. But what if you don't?"

The thrumming was a thunder in her head. "Are you just trying to scare me?"

"I'm saying all that might go away, and we could maybe work something out. But only if you tell us what you can and don't leave anything out." The pad was back in his hands, but Mr. Martinez wasn't writing. "We need to start with Mrs. Flanders and her house, talk about how you've been getting by these past few months. We also need you to make a statement about Patrick and his assault. And then we need to talk about Emily Burns."

The pressure in her head cracked, and she closed her eyes to swallow a sudden surge of nausea. She could see bright red hair and smell the glue of acrylic nails; dirt tucked into the creases of elbows and the folds of loose clothes; bloody sneakers and the stench of bleach. The great burning fire, burning her from the inside out. She whispered nonsense into her hair. "I don't know who that is."

Mr. Martinez, pen in hand, was steady and certain. "Yes, you do."

The lab was finally able to get a DNA sample from the girl; Martinez was fairly certain that the hair on the scrunchie would be Daisy's and would therefore be inconsequential, but that wasn't the source of his anticipation. The department had been given a gift—most of the material was entirely salvageable and, if they were lucky, the prints they found would match their predictions, finally giving them a bargaining chip to work with.

Martinez left Daisy detained in the interrogation room after two sharp knocks signaled him out. It was all spread out for him in the next room, the Chief sitting staunchly and scanning paperwork, van Daan moving from one side of the table to the next with a glib, unhealthy smile hooked onto his mouth.

Nature and the elements had been unforgiving hostesses, but the team in the lab had worked hard to recover what they could. The prints on the compact were inconclusive, and the hair found on the scrunchie was neither Emily's nor Daisy's. Martinez noted that and reached for the photos that could be scrounged from the films he'd uncovered. Three undeveloped film cartridges—what were the odds? But they'd been swaddled in that plastic bag; them, and a pair of cheap knock-off diamond earrings.

"No DNA, no prints. Kind of useless, these little mementos. Maybe she's just a bad thief, and this is her way of making returns."

"Indubitably, Daan." The Chief spoke like he was comforting an annoying child.

"But those earrings are tacky as hell. Tried to give Marlene a pair like that one year for Valentine's and we couldn't even get to the restaurant for dinner before she strong-armed me back to Zale's."

"That's because you're a cheap bastard, Daan."

Martinez ignored the banter. The anticipation he'd felt waiting on the results was fueled entirely by how much stock he'd placed on his hunch. It had driven him to haunt the lot, little more than a forsaken sandbox hunting for breadcrumbs from a stuttering, fumbling, abused ball of nerves edging towards a meltdown in the next room. He could proffer nothing else after this: Most of the photos were of random places outdoors, and Daisy, clearly the photographer, was in a scant handful of the pictures.

One shot in particular became his dark horse. Blurred at the edges, captured in motion, Emily Burns was sitting shotgun in a car, and a boy with thin, swathed black hair and a glinting nose ring was driving. They were twisted back in their seats and facing the camera head-on, a teasing grin on Emily's face. Daisy, her eyes bright, tufts of her hair fanning her face could be seen partially in the reflection of the rearview mirror. There was another figure in that car, sharing the backseat with Daisy but the face was obscured. Only the hand gripping the passenger headrest made fleshy by dark-red nail polish made Martinez aware of her presence in the car. He had met all of Emily's supposed friends, and these were strangers to him.

"The DNA test was a bust." Martinez studied a picture of a tabby cat lounging on a sidewalk slab. "These pictures are the best bet we got. But look at this one." He held up the picture of the car ride. "There's the two of them. There's no way for her to get out of this one. We show this to her, tell her we have more where it came from and we know about everything; this is our trump card."

The Chief nodded. "She's going to lie to you because she's scared. Treat it like a story and have her be the one to tell it. Do *not* threaten or pull out the intimidation—not unless you have to. Remember that she's just a kid." He paused, and then said, "You're on the right track. We'll see what happens now."

Martinez nodded and gathered up all the photos. He put his prize at the bottom of the stack and grabbed all the artifacts, bagged and labeled now. He would show them to her one at a time and draw her in. She had taken an immediate dislike to van Daan, so Martinez would come in alone and be a comfort rather than an adversary. He would gain her trust; she would see him as a confidante, a friend in the midst of the mess she was in.

He went in quietly, and she turned to him with wide eyes. He smiled gently and moved leisurely to his seat. "Your mother is here. I know you're pretty anxious to see her, but we need to clear the air first. Okay? Take a look at these."

By the time the Hispanic cop—Martinez, the first time she asked, and then later, Leonard—laid out the third photo, Daisy couldn't control the shakes. The cops had taken it—had taken *everything*. She should've guessed that a plan had been in play the second they brought her in.

If it had just been about Patrick, they would've let her go by now. Cops don't ever ask questions they don't already have the answers to. She had been assaulted by Patrick, almost *violated*. Patrick, who smelled like bologna on a good day and sounded like he was coughing when he laughed; Patrick, who his mother had once described to Daisy as "an infinite loser." If she was only a victim and nothing else, they would have let her out of the room they'd quarantined her in. They would at least have let her see her mother. She would have been consoled, counseled, swathed in temporary affection and promises for vengeance.

She was innocent, after all.

The topic had come up, her getting cornered by cops. Cops who heard gossip and showed up in places unexpectedly. She'd been given the gamut of advice: give a fake name, fake phone number and address, demand a lawyer, refuse to answer anything, deny everything. These tenets had been told to her before, and a grand daydream had taken root in her mind when she imagined her interrogation. She had expected it—anticipated it, even. She'd envisioned being resilient and levelheaded, outwitting her oppressors and evaded their aggressive gestures, escaping only just to run laughing in the night.

But she was tired, cold, thirsty (but unwilling to voice it), and drained of any willpower or defiance. All of her prepping had proven useless, and she wondered when, if ever, the control had shifted from her to this cop—she called him a cop, he called himself a *detective*—who sat before her as calm and steady as when she first came in. This cop who laid out the scrunchie, the compact, the earrings, and the photos and told her he needed her to be honest and sounded like he already knew she would lie.

"Listen. At this point it's pretty obvious that there's a lot we need to talk about. Why don't we just start at the beginning, hmm? Starting with your mom relocating to Halbart. We could probably start even before that."

She coughed weakly. "Can I see my mother?"

"Just as soon as we get this all sorted out," he said. "Your mother's waiting out in the lobby." He waited a beat, and then: "She had nothing but praise for you."

She wanted to scoff; before she could, a shrill whimper of a laugh came unbidden from her. "Did she really?"

"Yes. She said you were smart, skipped a grade already. Said you were very mature for your age and she never worried about you getting mixed up in the wrong things." The cop—Leonard, *Martinez*—crossed his arms and leaned back. "Are you going to let her down? Prove her wrong?"

When she said nothing, he asked her again. "Are you ready to begin?"

Daisy took a deep breath and held it. Each breath she took in succession was slower than the last, until at last her heartbeat dragged in her chest and smoothed into a slow cadence. Too many words and not enough time; they lay stillborn in her throat. Martinez waited patiently.

PART TWO

APRIL

SISSY TOMPKINS WAS HAVING A birthday party on Sunday, and a few of the girls from English and social studies were going to spend the night. Daisy sat behind Sissy in pre-algebra during seventh period. She was a loud, homely girl who snuck crackers and chips into class; once or twice she and Daisy had commiserated over Mr. Toor's love of pop quizzes and political cartoons. Sissy made a big show of inviting Daisy to the party and the sleepover after when they sat together at lunch, and Daisy contemplated attending either on the walk home from that day.

It wasn't that she didn't like Sissy. She wasn't particularly *fond* of her, but this was inconsequential: No one in her class was really friends. They turned on one another from one week to the next. It happened so often that Daisy hadn't even gotten upset when she found a dirty note about her written in a cursive print she recognized as belonging to her lab partner Janet Pinkerman scrawled down the wall of the girl's bathroom on the second floor. Janet, who just that month had looped arms with Daisy in the hallway after they'd presented their project and shared the makeup she'd swiped from her mother to paint Daisy's face after gym.

No, Daisy was hesitant to even show up at Sissy's house because she wouldn't have a gift and she didn't own a sleeping bag. It seemed bad planning to arrive and, when the other girls noticed her worn school backpack packed with a blanket, pillow, clothes and a homemade card, admit that she couldn't afford more. The girls would feign understanding to her face, but their whole class would know first thing Monday morning. For all the money that the youth of Pleasantville didn't have in comparison to the rest of the city, anyone that had even less was treated with scathing, disdainful pity that made Daisy's insides churn when she imagined it. She'd rather be mistaken for a snooty bitch than identified correctly, as poor white trash.

By the time she reached her front stoop, her mind was made up: She would beg off going, and on Monday she'd say it was because she'd been grounded for the weekend. For a moment, she paused and thought about all the food, the movies and the gossip—the simple sights and smells of *fun*—but this she shoved away forcefully as she found her key and let herself inside

The smell of her mother's new craze—scented candles—bombarded her immediately. For the past two weeks, she'd kept one burning at all hours of the day, right up until they would retire for the night, when the candle would be mercifully blown out. The candles were cheap, and the wax coating them was exceptionally oily, and the closer to the last dregs they burned, the more they took on an odor of melting plastic.

Still, Daisy was committed to not admitting how much she hated them. She accompanied her mother on her trips to the corner store, and with the potato flakes, bread, canned meat, and teabags came two, three, sometimes four of the store-brand candles that Daisy knew represented her mother's efforts to "make good" for them. Lately, her mother showed favor toward the plum-colored Sweet Sunshine Sage and always bought one whenever they got groceries.

What a stupid name for a candle. But Daisy still always went and retrieved it when her mother asked.

Her mother had not found steady work yet. It had been three months, and the unemployment checks were going to run out soon. They had already lost the cable and the gas—*it's too warm for that anyway, what an unnecessary cost*—and now, every day, upon getting up in the morning and coming home from school, the first thing Daisy did was check to make sure the lights still came on, the refrigerator was still running, the faucets still ran water. Coming inside today, she noted the dark of the living room and hurried on. She threw her backpack on the bed and rushed to the lamp on her bedside table. When the light came on, sickly and yellow, she sighed in relief. She turned the lamp off and shuffled into the kitchen.

Her mother had warned off using the electricity too much, so everything was turned off in the unoccupied rooms, and Daisy made a point of finishing her homework before the sun set. Tonight, she had reading assignments in English and notes to complete a presentation in speech—easy enough to do.

She poured a glass of water from the sink and drank slowly, contemplating food for dinner and breakfast the next morning. Draining the glass, she set it aside and ambled down the hallway to the voices she heard at the other end of the house.

Her mother was lying on the bed in the hazy dark of the early afternoon, still in her pajamas, watching a game show. She wasn't tucked into the blankets, which meant she'd gotten out of bed at some point. Daisy waited for the show to give way to a commercial break before going over and lying down delicately across the bed. They hummed their hellos.

"Afternoon, pumpkin." Her mother wrapped an arm and leg around her and hugged her tightly from behind. "You just get in?" Daisy nodded and relaxed as she felt a hand scratching lightly down her back. They watched commercials in a comfortable silence, and Daisy entertained the notion of a nap without closing her eyes. She stared at the television and waited for her mother to nudge her gently to get her to talk.

"School was good today." The show was back on, and the contestant was overweight and floundering on the obstacle course. She fell on her side, and the judges covered their laughter behind their hands. "Kind of ready for it to be the weekend, though." They'd had pizza as the main dish for lunch at school, just like every other Friday. Pizza with a fruit cup and chocolate pudding. Remembering made her contemplate the contents of their pantry again. "How was your day?"

Her mother rolled back and cat-stretched languorously behind her. "Oh, you know me. Pretty typical Friday. I really think that little old man down the street is dead, because I haven't seen him all week and that woman was back in his house. I saw her around noon when I was smoking. I bet she's his daughter. Pretty sad."

Daisy hummed and rolled onto her stomach. "Do we still have some of that chicken pasta?" Her mother was a wall of heat beside her, and she wanted to move away. Why had she asked about leftovers? They both knew there were none. "We could have that for dinner tonight."

"Actually, I thought we might get a pizza tonight." Her mother moved suddenly, rolled to her stomach until she was pressed to Daisy from head to toe and threw an arm across her. Daisy was reminded, suddenly, of how she loved her mother, and was never more aware of it than in the moments like this; loved how girlish and carefree she could be. Those were the moments that made Daisy feel girlish and carefree too. "C'mon. You didn't even ask me if anything new happened to me today."

"All right," Daisy said evenly. "Did anything new happen to you today?" Maybe they could get a deep-dish pizza with extra cheese. Pepperoni with mushrooms and a liter of soda—absolute bliss.

"Well," her mother dragged the syllable out, savoring the word like candy, "I finally got a call back on an application I put out last week."

Daisy breathed in and imagined the musty smell of the stained sheets beneath her as latent possibility. "Oh, really?" she said. "Which one?"

"Maid job. You know the new Hampton they built off the freeway? The manager left a voicemail and said they're 'aggressively seeking new people to add to the team.' God, corporate shtick is such a joke. Don't you think so?" Her mother laughed brightly and sobered quickly. "Of course, they always do that spiel. But who knows? This could be the break I've been looking for. We'll just have to see, hmm?"

Daisy nodded and kept silent. The phantom taste of pizza made her mouth water.

Sissy was completely unfazed by Daisy's apologies when she was finally able to get a minute alone with her. "Ah, don't worry about it. I got my ass handed to me after April knocked over one of my mom's angel figures she kept in the kitchen. That bitch had the nerve to say I pushed her into it. Can you believe that?"

The school year was nearly over. The end of junior high was rough, and across the eighth-grade wing of Pleasantville Junior High, students were sizing up the year that lay ahead of them. The majority of them would make the transition to the local high school. This was a given; at this point it was much more interesting to discuss which of them wouldn't be going to Pleasantville High, and for what reason. Some of them were moving out of town, and some of them, like the Selma twins, were moving to nicer neighborhoods and nicer schools. Some of them weren't going to Sweet Valley High because Sweet Valley High would not have them, a concept Daisy inwardly marveled over. What kind of kid could be so deplorable that the poorest school district in the county wouldn't accept them?

"Well, you know that girl in gym that used to sit on the side? She got pregnant in the boy's bathroom. Yeah, and the dad? He's getting kicked out too. They're going to have to go to Golden Hill."

Golden Hill was Sweetwater's only alternative school, planted outside the city limits and set up like a prison. Everything about Golden Hill was designed to be imposing. The students filling those halls were "criminals and total basket cases, man. I mean, they have bars on the *bathroom windows*. They lock those kids in there like animals. It's sick, really."

Occasionally, a commercial for the school would declare it "an effective institution enriching lives for the better;" but the soft music and angled shots did nothing to make the school seem any more welcoming. Daisy, gladly, would be going to Pleasantville High.

Before going through orientation and joining the ranks of incoming freshmen, there was the issue of the upcoming summer and making plans together for what seemed like the last time. Summer jobs, camps, vacations— but there was a league of kids just like Daisy who would slink around the neighborhood and dodge the creepers until the school year returned and brought normalcy back.

There had been one year, right before Daisy had started middle school, when she and her mother had gone for a weekend to the lake, the first and only trip they'd ever taken. They had driven in their car and hadn't broken down once, slept in the backseat swaddled in blankets under the stars, fished on the dock. They hadn't caught anything but mosquitoes. But before the long drive home, they ate at a diner. They got ice cream and ate it first, just like in the movies, and her mother had looked at her and said, "You are the best thing in my life."

Daisy imagined that experience, the scent of warm air and a night that belonged solely to them, and nothing had ever been more effortless. She remembered her mother's old job at the hospital; she could still taste the pilfered office suckers and hear the rubber shoes on the tile floor; closing her arms and reaching around herself, she recalled the feeling of tired arms that still tightened in at the end of the day.

Her mother had scheduled an interview for the maid job and had been alight ever since. "I'm going to show up ten, no, *twenty* minutes early. I need a new pair of shoes. Hotels always have a clear chain of command and built-in promotion schedules. Did you know that? Channel 9 said that. We'll even get discounts at the hotel too. Won't that be nice? To stay at the Hampton?"

It was hard to know which of them wanted her to get the job more. Daisy could only guess at their prospects for the summer if she didn't: crackers and cracked peppers, wilted salad and bruised bread from the food bank, bugs squirming in the floorboards. If the rains came early, it would mean building a nest of blankets in the living room for warmth and waiting, shivering, for the school to open its doors again.

Daisy promised her mother that she would get up early and make breakfast the day of her interview. Anything to help her succeed.

MAY

HER MOTHER GOT THE JOB, but it was only part-time. They celebrated it for the victory it was and talked for long hours about all the things they would buy. She worked late shifts and came home talking about the other maids, the front desk clerks, and the tragedies that played out in the messy sprawls of high-priced rooms. She declared again and again that people's lives were best captured in the trash they threw away. "That's why I'm so proud of us, sweet pea. We don't have much, but we live clean. We have it all right."

Daisy nodded and tutted and busied herself with housework. Her mother was working again, so she did chores and made simple meals, focusing on her tasks to keep her surging hopes in check.

In a few weeks, the school year would be over and Daisy would graduate from junior high. Posters lined the halls announcing the upcoming exodus. The school sent notices in the mail inviting the community to the ceremony. A student committee was chosen to decorate the gym for the after-party, their last school dance. Having patched things over with her mother, Sissy confessed over lunch that she would be throwing a sendoff sleepover following the festivities. "And I'm not taking no for an answer this time, Miss Daisy Mae." Sissy glared at her across the table, and since Sissy knew Daisy hated the nickname, she glared steadily back. "You just stay out of trouble that weekend, hear? It's my last party before the summer comes."

It was that sentiment, coupled with the palpable thrum of excitement that pervaded every corner of the school, that Daisy couldn't help but succumb to, and she promised she would come and even felt the small prickles of excitement at the prospect. The last party she would attend as an eighth grader—that was as special an occasion as any she'd ever had. On warm afternoons by the open window in her math class, Daisy marveled at her good fortune: Her mother had a steady job now; she could probably ask for a sleeping bag now without causing a fuss.

A sleeping bag: durable and soft and a symbol of good living.

It was a small pink one she had had her eye on. But when she asked, her mother scoffed and said it was too expensive. "Can't you just take a blanket? Or borrow one from a friend?"

Daisy had timed her request down to the day she knew her mother was paid and had been home long enough to unwind from work. Sitting next to her on their splotched green couch, her mother was saying no and sounding final. There was exactly one week left until graduation and subsequently the sleepover and the applesauce jar under her bed had three dollars, some change, and an old jacket button.

How was she going to get forty dollars in one week? Dog-walking, mowing lawns, lemonade stands—those were things kids living past the east highway did. Who in her neighborhood would give an odd job worth that kind of cash to a twelve-year-old girl?

"Baby, baby," her mother crooned, reaching over to ruffle her hair, "it's just a party. No one's going to care. You are going to have such a good time, and this isn't even going to matter."

With nothing else to say—and a little too proud to beg—she simply agreed and smiled wanly when her mother looked over. They had cold cuts and sweet tea for dinner, and she slunk away early to bed, saying she had a headache and a quiz first thing the next morning. With her window and the door closed, the room was too warm, and she thrashed irritably in her trundle bed.

Boys in her class sometimes talked about a scrap yard on the far end of the neighborhood and hidden behind the overpass. The owner was supposedly a reticent old bachelor who paid cash for salvageable car parts and metals. It was a five-mile walk one way, and she would only be able to lessen that distance by cutting through the alleys and fields in between, a dangerous venture. But if she left directly after school, she could get there in time to beat the early afternoon traffic, and that might help to stave off ill-meaning strangers. She would call her mother from the office phone and tell her she was going to stop at a friend's house.

Her plan soothed her. She settled herself and closed her eyes.

The wind that day was unseasonably fierce. It seemed to change directions with every step she took and slowed her down. Although it buffeted her hair and swept dirt in her eyes, blinding and frustrating her, she was grateful for the cool air. The sun above was vengeful, and the only clean shirt she'd found that morning was long sleeved. She'd set out from the school in a rush, not letting herself hesitate. She'd been doggedly persistent for the first two miles, but after four the only thing keeping her going was the fear of turning back empty-handed.

Her biggest fear had been being seen by her classmates during her trek. Kids talked about each other, all the time, the moment they noticed something, anything suspicious in the least. She knew this and accepted it like any other decision that had been made for her, but even decisions made for her could prove unfortunate. A friend, possibly sailing past her in a car with a parent or pedaling a bike or skateboard, might see her, scuffed all to hell with her unwashed hair a mesh net in the wind, going far out of her way with her school gear in the blazing heat headed…somewhere. Then people would start asking questions she couldn't answer—questions like, where did she live? Where was she going? And soon the terrible truth would come out—because what else could she tell them?

Especially when she'd have to explain how she got the metal scraps—or the cash.

She had tried to find an alternative. Checking on her own block and alley had been a complete waste of time; it was a compound bed of dirt and shit and odd strips of cloth and old, godforsaken debris, but none of the copper or aluminum or, God forbid, soda cans that could be cashed in.

As far as she knew, the only way to get the right materials would be to jump the fences of the derelict properties she could reach and just dig in, root around until she found something worthwhile, stuff it in her bag—emptied, light on her back, all her school supplies safe in her locker at school—and make a run for it, lest the homeowner spot her. That's how the boys in her class did it. Going out in trios, four or five, always a pack; they never went out alone because you never knew when you'd need to split and flee, or when you'd discover too much for one person to haul off.

She wouldn't have that issue, she told herself, because she didn't need much. But before any of this, of course, she needed to talk to the man who owned the scrap yard. To a Mr. Bobby Jung.

One foot in front of the other. Beside her, on either side of the highway, golden stretches of scorched, sun-starched grass blew and flapped in the hot wind, rolling and undulating like waves of a burning ocean. Back and forth, moving with the tide of the breeze; she breathed in through her nose, burned her nostrils, opened her mouth and tasted the salty earth and gulped it down, though it held no sustenance. She tried to walk in shadowed area,s but there was absolutely no shade to head toward. She wished for water and tried not to think about having to wait until she finally got home to have some. Wondering how she was going to conduct herself with Mr. Jung and trying not to sound like an intimidated idiot occupied her focus.

Walking through the alleys to cut the distance gave her the added benefit of cover while she traveled but had done nothing to assuage her paranoia during her journey. The effect was quite the opposite: The wind carried voices, lowered and raised, ageless and genderless, dogs barking, yipping and snarling, cars speeding up and slowing down, the alarming echo of glass shattering and sirens wailing down the highway. She felt hunted and betrayed even with no one else around. She dredged up the last reserves of her energy and tried to ignore the sweat that puddled on her.

When she finally crossed over the intersection and saw the little red house in the stretch, it was a blessing. The last mile was nearly under way, and it couldn't have taken her longer than an hour. She hurried on with renewed vigor and rehearsed her introduction. *My name is Daisy, and I heard you were looking for parts.*

Short, polite, and direct. That was the best way to do this. She wouldn't need to tell him a story or make it personal or linger on—one and done, and then never again. And she would go to the store on Friday alone, give her mother some excuse: get the sleeping bag and keep it in her locker, bring it home after the school year was over and the whole thing became an afterthought. Her mother would forget her asking for a sleeping bag, like she forgot about everything else. "Oh, this? Sissy had a spare. She said I could have it, you know, for next time. I know, it was very nice of her." Easy as breathing.

She walked on a dirt strip along the road as she got closer and noted the absence of any other houses nearby. Jung's Scraps and Supplies lay in a secluded part of the area. There was a clear division: While the valley was densely populated, houses tended to nestle in one corner and business in another. Mr. Jung's place was different in that his business was away from anything and anyone else, and it was understood that he lived on the property. No wife, no kids; the boys in Daisy's class said he wasn't right in the head, but Daisy shoved that thought away.

Short, polite, direct: no need to get personal or share sob stories. No need to, because this wasn't going to be a regular thing.

Jung's setup was a dirt yard with structures of all configurations gleaming in the sun. The office and house lay off to the right corner, and despite the piles of sad scraps stranded across the lot, the paint on the house was fresh and whole. Despite missing a few letters, the business sign was polished and prominent.

It was not until she was too close to turn back that she saw there were figures prowling across the yard that Daisy distinguished as kids—teenagers, not from her school, and Daisy didn't recognize them—but no Jung in sight. Daisy faltered. It was two boys and a girl, and while the boys were dressed simply in jeans and T-shirts, the girl was clad completely in black; *jet* black and long sleeved, not an inch of skin exposed. She was pale, and her long neck swooped up to a full head of bright red hair that fell unevenly about her face. She and the boys were moving about and completely unconscious of her, so Daisy stood still and watched them as they seemed to stroll casually around the scrap yard. They were not reaching out and touching things, and they were not talking, either. Rather, they were spread out, eyes to the ground and the piles surrounding them, assessing slowly and carefully. Daisy watched them in the heat and ignored the way the sweat ran in her eyes. Instead, she favored the apprehension creeping over her as she lingered in place. Going another step and entering the compound was unthinkable. The nerves in her stomach strangled her; she wanted to turn around and just go home, just take the loss and try again later.

At some point the haze dispersed. She was peeling the damp hair off her neck and the trio was reconvening again and making to leave. Jung hadn't come out the entire time. Was he even home? Was that why these strangers moved like they owned the place? There were no trees for her to duck behind, and she began walking again, casual as she could, *nothing to see here*, and it was for naught. The trio never looked at her. They turned as one and walked past the house to the back fence as serenely as they'd come. The barbed wire was rusted and hung low—one of the boys graciously held the wire down with his foot while the girl climbed over—and they were walking up the hill and out of sight.

The gate door had no lock and opened easily to her trembling hands. She had come all this way, sweating and dizzying herself under the afternoon sun, and she was going to at least knock on the door, damn it. And suddenly she was at the door, noting the dirt and the stains. It opened and there was Mr. Jung, with a scowling, suspicious expression.

David Jung was forty-five and, as the boys from Daisy's school had described him, soft in the head and wary of everything. He had black hair peppered in with gray, buzzed close to his head in a military style. His eyes were a dull brown and his jaw hung from his face. She noted that although his hands were dirty and his clothes were stained, his shirt was tucked into his pants and the collar of his shirt had been ironed. Oddly enough, his cheeks were ruddy and pink just like a little boy's. Daisy thought he looked like a little boy who had simply never grown up.

"You here for—what you here for?"

Daisy blinked and took a step back. The smell of him washed over her. "I-I'm Daisy. Kids at my school said you need parts. Do you…need parts?"

He shook his head and scrunched his face. "You mean what? Where the kids at your school?"

"They said that you—Tommy. Tommy and Andrew. Do you know them?" Her face was burning under her blush, and she was fidgeting. He was tracking her movements with a singular focus that unnerved her. "They said they'd been here before."

"Tommy and Andrew," he said slowly. "Tommy and Andrew? You know them?" He was staring at her as if he could see inside her and she wanted to run. Stupid stupid *stupid*. Tommy and Andrew were dirty liars. Practically the scum of the earth. "The parts you bring? From school?" He said it incredulously, as if she were out of her mind.

She looked at him and saw that his hair was combed, but his clothes were dirty and torn; that his house, from over his shoulder, was dark and hardly a shell of an office; and she knew with certainty that the boys at her school were cruel beyond measure, and so was she. "Yes," she said evenly. "I bring the parts from school. Do you need parts from school?"

His expression cleared, and in his open face Daisy found trust. All at once he was friendly and jovial and she smiled to encourage him. "Okay, good. Parts on Tuesdays, coppers on Thursdays, the metals on Fridays. See you soon?" And he held out his hands for hers. She put her hands in his and shook both at once. He beamed and nodded at her and quickly turned to go back inside. The entire meeting couldn't have been longer than ten minutes.

It was a victory only in that it was over quickly. She had gotten what she wanted without a particular struggle, and she felt raw about it. But it didn't matter. A verbal contract had been made, and she would deliver. Thursday she could come back with copper. She would thank Mr. Jung and wish him well. One and done. Easy as breathing.

"And so you just—what? Where'd you get the copper?"

"I didn't get any real copper. Or it was—I don't know. I don't think it was real copper, but it was a bunch of blocks and, like, pieces. I pulled it from someone's yard."

"Did you receive any compensation form Mr. Jung for it?"

"Yeah. Twenty dollars."

"Was it just the one and done after all?"

She paused. "No. I went about seven or eight times."

"Were you always paid in cash for these transactions?"

"Yes."

"And did you always go alone?"

"Yes."

"Could you not have—sorry." He leaned back, cleared his throat, and leaned forward again. "Did you not ever consider how dangerous an activity that is? Just scrapping metal you happen to find? You could've been kidnapped... attacked. That's not even mentioning that it's stealing. What if someone had seen you on the road?"

"I know that, okay? I know all that. I just needed money. There was no other way for me to get it. Besides, my mom ended up losing that job at the hotel. They fired her."

"Did you mother know about the scrapyard?"

"No. And it didn't matter; she ended up having to go to Halbart anyway."

"Why did your mother have to go to Halbart?"

"To help my grandmother."

She didn't end up earning enough money for her sleeping bag in time to use it. And as she'd feared, the girls did snicker and whisper. They plucked at her things with nimble fingers and kicked them to the floor dismissively. It didn't matter; the closer she came to the last day of school, the more optimistic she felt. She spent the money she earned and bought a new blanket instead, and on the last day of school she packed her backpack with a flourish. Her mother greeted her with oatmeal and coffee, and they sat together at the table before she got dressed.

Her favorite breakfast with her mother on her favorite day of the year put an extra spring in her step. They laughed together, and her mother told her that she looked like she was on the moon. Her mother bragged about how she'd impressed her shift manager in the past week, and Daisy promised she would clean the house before the end of the weekend. She dressed quickly and flew out of the house, chiding herself to stop from running to school, embarrassed for being so anxious to begin the day.

The hallways were overrun with posters and students and yearbooks and markers and voices; voices calling and crying, cheering and jeering, flooding across the corridors. The principal said they were the best eighth-grade class the school ever had, and the students accepted it with good humor. Daisy's angry, churlish PE coach hugged her goodbye; her English teacher conducted their last class outdoors. At lunch, water balloons were conjured and pelted across the courtyard with abandon. Daisy laughed and laughed and laughed again until she thought she would choke. "Makes you wonder how awesome high school will be," Amelia White crooned, and she and Daisy shared a smile.

The dance was a swarm of dark light and grabbing, twisting bodies in every direction. Hands, weaving over the crests of her breasts, the hollows of her hips, snagging in her hair. *Sorry*, hissed a voice in the throng as friends led her deeper into the mass. Their gym was cheaply and inadequately decorated; she and the girls disparaged the school board and PTA staff for creating a kingdom so below their station. They walked lightly and with measured steps, as if they were the main attraction in the promenade.

Daisy said she did not want to dance, and the others didn't push. Only so many times could she and her friends clutch and roll against one another before a nearby boy would leer and make crude comments about "butch bombshells" and "dirty bitches", and they would wrench apart in a flurry. The boundaries the girls and boys used to separate themselves from each other, once clearly so drawn and immovable, were now blurred and dismissible. And Sissy, who had most vehemently insisted that Daisy come out to partake of the festivities, was the first to vanish into the throng in the company of some boy—some *boy* with the seeds of acne scars planted in his face, who held her not by the hand but by the forearm and dragged her away without a backward glance.

They left eventually. Sissy's house was an arduous seven blocks away. They huddled together and sloshed their way down the cracked, puddled sidewalks like drunken fools, the pock-marked, hair-slicked boys of their homeroom class in tow. The front door was unlocked with no car in the driveway. Sissy's house could always be counted on to have a bounty of cheap junk food and expendable upholstery. They busted open the kitchen cabinets, and the celebration began anew.

At some point, music floated down from Sissy's bedroom from behind a closed door. It cut through the roar of activity that diluted Daisy's sense of time and responsibility. She noticed then that Sissy and the boy were gone and couldn't recall exactly when it happened. With a fresh bag of chips smuggled away, Daisy cut a slow stroll to the back door and waited for the television to transition to commercials before ducking back into darkness.

The full moon was enough to keep her cheerful as she darted along, wanting to hum but also wanting to stay invisible. Not a bad night, all things considered. Sissy's parties weren't all that bad, if you remembered that for all her pretenses and cheerful demeanor, Sissy's family was as poor as any other in the valley. Sissy's father was an alcoholic who, while friendly and affable enough, would wander up and down their block in his underwear, sometimes singing or caroling and always so gleeful about it. Her mother was a salted crust of a woman who won $53,000 in a lawsuit for a fall she'd suffered in a grocery store during a pregnancy, and for all anyone knew the family was still living off that settlement.

The Tompkins weren't unique in their poverty, but not everybody in the neighborhood was so bad off. There was Jonathan Tremble and his family: He was a star student, shared the girls' math class, and always took advantage of first year introductions to brag about his annual summer vacation. He was raised by his mother and sister, and they both worked full-time. Sissy, for all that she claimed to have, couldn't claim that.

Daisy did not see herself as particularly unfortunate, but some people were simply luckier.

The darkness made everything seem infinite. She could've stayed outside the entire night, after all the effort she'd gone through to enjoy the outing, but it was one thing to make like she was carefree and another thing entirely to be careless. She was airy enough as she side-stepped grooves and trash wrappers in her path, the moon casting a cold glow on everything she saw.

What time was it? She didn't know. It had been fairly late when she and the others set out from the school to walk home. They were a pack then, and Daisy was reminded starkly of her aloneness. The severity of it crystalized when she saw Bobby Jenkins appear ahead of her on the sidewalk.

Bobby Jenkins was a grotesque figure; grotesque because the arrangement of his features had the power to unsettle anyone. Standing in the sunlight was not enough to dispel the shadow that seemed to shift over him like a second skin. All of the kids in Daisy's circle knew him. As sixth graders, they watched him stroll up the block during their free period, smoking cigarettes and waving jauntily at them as he strode by, thin, birdlike and shirtless, pants weighted down by the tall boys jammed into his back pockets.

Supposedly he had a fiancée that lived just outside the valley, and Jenkins made the trek each day over the overpass to see her. They were lovers and business partners of some sort. Every now and again he could be seen driving a half-dead pickup around with her in the front seat, loading and unloading and reloading televisions from unknown sources. The fiancée was an old student of Pleasantville High. Had she graduated? Probably not. *Have you seen her? She looks like she's twelve. A crack whore and a pedophile—what a pair.*

Daisy stopped as soon as she was too close to pretend he wasn't there; he didn't move, and neither did she. They were frozen in place. He only appeared to be standing on the pavement. On a night with no cars streaming by, no raucous laughter and no sirens, it felt like a barrier had been breached as she rocked on the heels of her feet. He was facing her, and they were close enough to hear each other speak, but he said nothing.

"How's it going." It was the first time she'd ever spoken to him.

He did not respond, and Daisy doubted that he'd even understood her. His head was cocked to the side ,and he was listening—to her or something else. She listened too, but he was hearing something she could not. She doubted she could pass him without him trying to touch her, and she made to cross to the other side of the street when his body canted toward her. In the illuminating moonlight she saw half of his face, enough to see that he was gazing at her—into her, through her, pinning her in place.

"You shouldn't be out here alone. Ever," he said. "None of you should." And then he calmly turned around and went back the way he came. When he was fully engulfed in the darkness Daisy could've sworn she heard him break into the pat-pat pounding of a sprint. She herself lumbered home in a daze.

When she finally got to her house, she was expecting it to be empty, but the lights were on and her mother was seated at the kitchen table. She was sitting as if anticipating Daisy's arrival and waited for Daisy to sit down gingerly before clearing her throat.

"What has happened?" Daisy asked.

Her mother sighed. "It's Nana, dear. Oh, baby. I'm so sorry."

"What exactly was it that happened to your nana?"

"She was in a home in Halbart. She fell out of bed and broke her hip at some point. It was a bunch of other stuff after that too. I think there was an infection or something."

"You say your mother left to help care for her?"

"She drove that night to Halbart to be with her. After a couple days she came back, and then it became, like, our new thing."

"What did you do in the meantime?"

"Just—whatever. Walked to school and kept up like everything was normal."

"And what did your mother say when she came back?"

"That Nana was near death, and the people at the home were forcing her to stay in bed. That's what caused it all; that they were trying to keep her doped up so she wouldn't be a bother. That she needed to keep a closer eye on Nana from now on."

"So then these trips began. Your mother going back and forth."

"Yeah, she wasn't gone all that much at first. Like, she would go over the weekend, come back, go the next weekend, come back. After a while it just got to be longer and longer."

"Were you always able to get by in her absence?"

"I'm not a baby." She lifted her chin. "I can do whatever I have to do."

"If that's the case, why did your mother approach Mrs. Flanders to look after you?"

"Because she thought I would be lonely. She didn't like me being in the house by myself, and Mrs. Flanders was in the neighborhood."

She hadn't been expecting her mother to be home by the time she got home from school. This wasn't the day they'd agreed she would come home.

Originally, they had struck a deal: Her mother would go and camp out over the weekend in Halbart, but she would be home in time to see her off to school Monday morning. They would have the week together, and she would continue to go to work. And Daisy may have wanted to protest or at least voice her doubts, but her mother was quick to assure her that it was all temporary, only temporary. Nana was sick, hopelessly, dreadfully sick. Her hip was shattered, and at her age she would never walk again. Her caretakers were dirty, cruel people who would starve her to death before they would treat her with dignity.

"I have to be with her while I still can, Daisy. For both of us—you can understand that, can't you?" And Daisy could remember on a single hand the number of times she'd ever met or spent time with her nana. She wasn't Daisy's grandmother, but Nana had raised her mother, and, "I just can't let her go out like that."

Her mother whispered her apologies into the bathroom sink, her back bowed to Daisy in the hallway, and the subject was closed.

Mrs. Flanders was a nice enough lady. Her house reeked of hand lotion and onions, an odd, disconcerting odor that caked the house and sometimes seeped out from under the closed doors. She had no cable or satellite television, so on the weekends she stayed over, Daisy lounged around on the living room sofa and kept the television trained on the local channels on a low volume through the long afternoons to distract herself from the mountains in her mind. She ate cereal in the mornings and waited for Mrs. Flanders to wobble in to the table so they could exchange pleasantries long enough that Daisy could then slip out into the neighborhood without feeling guilty.

Mrs. Flanders had once had a house crowded with children and had been an early widow. She told Daisy it was nice to have a young person in the house again, said the feeling hearkened back to an entirely different world. She anointed her as an addition to the family. "A girl too," the old woman warbled. "Before you, I had nothing but boys," and Daisy ignored the tremors in the hands that clasped her face.

It was an unspoken agreement that they would not talk about their new arrangement openly, Daisy and her mother. The school certainly didn't need to be involved, that much all parties agreed on. Waking up alone and eating a stranger's food, walking home and flitting through the days without contact— for the first few weeks, this charade went by smoothly enough. The stale, watery food was fine; the long silent stretches of neighborhood streets with no conversation was fine; the lack of a voice outside her own was even fine.

It was all fine, really.

JULY

EVENTUALLY, IT WASN'T QUITE FINE anymore.

Eventually her mother stopped coming home when they agreed she would. Sunday night one week, Tuesday afternoon the next. Food began to vanish faster than it was replaced, and clothes piled up around the house in inconvenient corners. Her mother was full of promises, always ready with some quip about the weather or some gossip carried on the winds, tireless in her efforts to fill up the silences with bright chatter.

Eventually, Daisy stopped listening.

They started having problems paying the bills again. It wasn't simply the lack of groceries: it became the lack of groceries, cable, air conditioning, electricity, water—everything. Eventually her mother let it slip that her unemployment payments were running out. "They let me go, dear, over some nonsense," her mother said. "They said they knew I was stealing the hotel supplies. Can you even imagine?"

Daisy began to look forward to the weekends she went over to Mrs. Flanders's house. It was the same lumpy sofa and the same nearly expired milk for cereal, but it was also a television without the fuzz and static, and a fan that could stay on all day. It was a half-hearted conversation, but a conversation outside the recesses of her meanderings, lonely and alone in the heat of the unforgiving summer.

Eventually, she learned to expect nothing more.

For the nights in between Mrs. Flanders's house and her own, when she couldn't settle herself, she took to the streets to explore the valley.

She wasn't alone. There was no time of day where she wouldn't find someone strolling the sidewalks of the neighborhood stricken with people and their diseases, but the streets got even more crowded at dusk. Some of them were night creepers who ran and bobbed and darted down the blocks, and others were drunken imbeciles struggling to crawl back to their burrows, like Amelia's father, and all the sagging, shapeless fathers like him. Their desperate march would lead them down the center of the road and risk the stray cars that lost their benevolence with the setting sun. Occasionally, Daisy saw dog walkers and dealers posted on corners, hugging the walls behind them and holding themselves like soldiers on post. The only ones who ever spoke to her were the painted women; unlike her, they were out to be seen.

It wasn't a regular thing, her wandering. Only on the evenings she couldn't sleep did she venture outside. And she wasn't stupid. Anyone with five minutes to spare had a story to tell of some young innocent who was in the wrong place at the wrong time and was punished by fate for their foolishness. Most of them were trumped up and fantastic, but she heeded their moral. She stuck to shadows, keeping an ear to the ground and an eye on the unfamiliar shapes in the deep darkness. Some nights she even found more metal scraps to salvage.

It was a bad thing to do, she knew, and she hadn't ever wanted to go back to Jung after the first visit. But, her mother had begun to drift away from her, away from their quiet little life. Mrs. Flanders wasn't a solution to her problem either, merely a thin bandage to cover the wound. She needed the scraps because she needed the money. On the evenings when she had made a good harvest and hiked the hills without any dangerous encounters, she climbed the steps of the valley's only Methodist church and watched the sun rise. It was a balm for her nerves, always churning beneath the surface.

That she would eventually spend every night out on her little quests was a seamless transition. It was the inevitable conclusion, to lose the little bit of high ground she had. It wasn't a sacrifice, either; there was no one in her life to even notice. One morning, toward the end of the month, she had been sneaking into her house for a change of clothes, and her mother rolled into the driveway just as she was jiggering the kitchen window open.

"What are you doing?" she heard just as she began hoisting herself up. She almost couldn't drop into a proper crouch without scraping her face against the wall panel. "It's a fine Wednesday morning, and you're breaking into our house?"

Daisy righted herself slowly. "Lost my house key. I thought you wouldn't be home until the weekend."

"Nana was feeling a little better this week. They got a new nurse, and I like her; she seems to have an excellent work ethic." As she got closer, Daisy could see her mother was holding her purse in one hand and a box of donuts in the other. "The maple ones are your favorite, right?"

Daisy nodded slowly and approached. When was the last time they'd had donuts? It was an unnecessary luxury, nixed a long time ago. When she reached for the box she could feel the warmth of the donuts' freshness wafting through the thin cardboard. She took a maple and cherry in one hand and handed the box back with the other, taking bites intermittently from each palm.

"So what are your plans for today? You want to go into town? We could drop our clothes off and go see a movie. I checked, and at the dollar theater they have—"

"Did you get paid? Is there a new job yet?" Her voice came out much harsher than she intended, but as she watched, her mother was slow to catch on to what Daisy was really asking: How were they going to afford this mother-daughter day?

But her mother just smiled enigmatically and kept the answer tucked behind her teeth. "Oh, don't worry; I won't run out. We're going to have fun today, aren't we? It's your summer vacation. We have to live it up."

And her mother turned around and retreated up the porch steps. She disappeared around the side of the house ,and Daisy listened for the front door to thud closed. She finished the last of her donuts and went gingerly inside.

They gathered up a third of the laundry marooned throughout the house with a sock full of quarters and corner-store detergent. For two hours they washed and waited in equal measure with minimal conversation. Her mother hugged her at every opportunity until eventually Daisy saw her coming in and put up an elbow—blocked her once, and that was that. They did go into town, and they did get groceries, and they did end up going to see that movie; but they did not hug, did not touch, and her mother did not call her pet names or talk about going to stay at the Hamptons or make her promises for the next day. Strangers did not live in debt to other strangers, so nothing real had been lost.

It was the end of the month when she saw the trio from outside Jung's again.

She was on another late night walk and had found old car parts—a muffler, maybe?— deposited beside a dumpster. It was on a block close to the freeway, and she had one ear to the irregular rhythm of traffic. She was struggling to get the grease off the contraption—a carburetor, had to be a carburetor—so she could get it in her backpack without it staining, when she turned and saw them standing together at the end of the street.

Interactions after dark had become more dangerous than in the previous weeks. Hands came out of nowhere some nights, in her hair, over her face and shoulders. They tightened and tried to pull her in, and she swung her bag until the hands retreated. She sprinted away as fast as she could, predatory laughter and incoherent catcalling following close behind.

Maybe it was the heat. The night air, warm and cloying, had borne a new host of faces she hadn't recognized from nights past. These newcomers jeered at her, circled her; they entreated her and tried to soothe her in tones she struggled to decode. It was on a night that she hadn't seen anyone—hadn't run into any threats, emboldening her to go outside her comfort zone—that she saw a glinting in the streetlight, recognized a head of shaggy red hair.

The quickest route back to her house was straight down the road toward the trio, who were full ensconced in the light, their faces shadowed. They stood facing her, unmoving and wordless, and they stayed still long enough for fear to infect her, and she could go no further. Daisy looked around and surveyed the houses. She could jump one of the fences and run, if need be. Would they pursue? She'd never seen them out at night before, and the air was hot and thick in her lungs. She blinked again and again to clear her vision.

She hadn't heard any dogs on the way, and the streets were empty of cars. She swallowed, gripped the straps of her bag and lurched forward. As she crossed the fence with less grace than usual, she could've sworn that a raspy, nasal voice said, "See you later," to her retreating back; she ran faster and pushed herself until she thought her chest would burst.

"Who are these kids you're talking about?"

"Jesus and Tommy, they're brothers. The girl is Avia."

"Avia?"

"It's short for something. She never said what."

"Classmates of yours?"

"No. Tommy was already graduated, Avia was a senior. I think Jesus dropped out."

"These kids live in the Valley?"

"They did, yeah."

"And how exactly did you come into association with them?"

"Avia is cousins with Patrick; Mrs. Flanders is her aunt."

"Really."

"Yeah, really. You know…you know what Mrs. Flanders told me about her?"

"What."

"She said that Avia had a bad experience as a child and almost died. She said it would've been better for her if she had."

AUGUST

SOMETIMES MRS. FLANDERS LOST HER sense of time and space.
As a recluse, there was no rhyme or reason to the routine of her life. A row of thin, outdated dresses lined her closet and were just for show; Mrs. Flanders only ever wore nightgowns now. Some days Daisy would come to spend the afternoons camped out on the couch with the window air conditioner cranked up as far as it would go, and had anyone asked, she would've said she was waiting for Mrs. Flanders to come down, but no one ever did. The front door was never locked, and she would let herself in to find Mrs. Flanders sitting at the table for who knew how long. Some days Daisy would come in and make as much noise as she could, dropping her bag with a clatter and stomping her feet, but still the old woman would startle when Daisy grabbed the crook of Mrs. Flanders's arm to help her back upstairs.

The nurse that came to the house was a fat Filipino named Ruth who came around on Wednesday mornings and smelled worse than Mrs. Flanders. Daisy avoided coming to the house on Wednesdays at all costs. Ruth pocketed random things in the house she wanted and deposited the junk she didn't. The only presence in the house that was more unsettling and pervasive was Patrick's. He tended to unstick himself from the ether and take refuge in his bedroom on Sundays.

Daisy avoided Sundays at the Flanders house at all costs too.

The nails on Patrick's fingers were black and had been for a long time. It was a side effect of drugs or disease, and it was impossible to discern which came first. He was middle-aged, now, a leering pervert of a man who stared a little too long and leaned a little too close. The timbre of his voice was ragged and hoarse. Like the unnatural orange of his hair, he shared his voice with the dying woman he studiously ignored. Maybe it was from a lifetime of screaming at each other, leaving them with no voices and no words in their old ages.

She had learned in the fifth grade that no one could look someone in the eye with both eyes at the same time, and that was especially true of Patrick, with his twitchy nature and flighty gestures. He disturbed her more than anyone she'd ever known.

On a Tuesday morning, she let herself in and grabbed the last pastry from the box on the kitchen table. She munched it slowly, noting its staleness and flipping through the channels on the television until she came to a show that wasn't a Spanish telenovela. The house was still and smelled oddly sweet. Ruth would have to take out the trash again and clean out the refrigerator too. How much laundry was there? Mrs. Flanders and Patrick both seemed to wear the same outfit every day. How many of her clothes could she fit into her backpack? Probably a week's worth, right? Maybe a towel or two? If she could find her book bag, she reasoned, she might be able to pack even more. Maybe if she put it directly at the bottom of the basket in the bathroom and scattered other pieces casually around the house, it would seem as though she were over more often, and then Ruth would have to include her things when she washed the bedding—

"My auntie said you were here sometimes. I thought she was just talking out of her ass again.'

Daisy's head snapped around so fast she gave herself whiplash. The girl with the dull red hair stood calmly in the doorway to the kitchen. She had been standing there watching Daisy for a while. Long enough, at least, to have procured a cup of coffee and the last apple Daisy had spied in the fruit bowl. With one hand, the girl held her food perfectly balanced while the other hand cocked a cigarette to her lips. Daisy had no idea how she hadn't smelled the smoke.

Her voice sounded ridiculous in her head. "You aren't supposed to smoke in the house."

The girl flicked the ashes of her cigarette onto the floor and kept her eyes trained on Daisy as she did so. "And that's a rule you know firsthand, because you've broken it before. Am I right?" Daisy did not respond, and the girl didn't press her to speak. It was a simple jab.

Eventually, the girl ducked back into the kitchen, and Daisy, not knowing what to do, turned around and resumed watching television. It was a documentary covering the history of a museum three states away and the narrator had a voice so gravelly that Daisy waited through the first commercial break and then turned the volume down for the rest of the broadcast.

She waited through an hour's worth of infomercials selling a multifaceted knife set before she ventured into the kitchen. The red-haired girl wasn't there. She wasn't lurking in the hallway or on the staircase either. Daisy listened hard and heard empty echoes before she made a sandwich and wolfed it down, standing up rigidly by the counter. She grabbed a pair of granola bars from the cupboard and left the house through the front door. She didn't need to be in the Flanders house that week. There were books she could read in her room to pass the time.

Hours later, she reconsidered. Waiting until Thursday to stop back by Mrs. Flanders's meant going a day and a half without food, so Daisy came in through the gate to the backyard at night and tried the side door to get in. The doorknob was so loose in its socket that Daisy almost tore it free. She huddled in the darkness before creeping forward. Her destination: the kitchen, maybe the bathroom, but only if the coast was clear.

She could clearly see the cast of the television on the walls of the hallway as she snuck a hand into the cupboard, the other hand holding onto the door hinge to silence it. Someone was in the living room, but the shadows were impossible to decipher from where she was standing. She grabbed a bag of chips—the cheap kind, Ruth did the shopping—and stuffed it quickly in her backpack. There would be no getting in the refrigerator tonight. She edged slowly to the back door when a peal of laughter erupted behind her.

The hallway was a narrow strip that sectioned off the separate quarters of the house. She was lingering near the mouth of the archway before she was aware of it. There was the skeleton of the staircase rail bouncing off the wall to her right; the sound of whispering and noises from the show was filtering in, and it was obvious to her now that whoever was watching television wasn't alone. She flattened herself against the wall and canted her head forward. She flinched at the sudden light that flooded her face.

It was the girl with the red hair, sitting on the couch between the two boys who'd been standing with her under the streetlight that night. For the first time Daisy noticed that one of the boys had long hair. The other boy had short, chopped hair gelled in spikes and a hand gripping the back of the girl's neck tightly; the other hand was clutching the television remote. They were watching a movie; a DVD player sat atop the television, along with a pile of bags that leaned against the wall by the front door.

Everything roared in Daisy's ears: the explosions coming from the television, the muttering from the longhaired boy, the other boy making faint grunting noises as the volume got hiked up, and the girl, the girl answering some question lost in the haze as she brushed hair out of her face, as she slowly turned her head.

Daisy's limbs felt heavy and lame as she backed away. She may have been loud as she wrenched open the back door and leapt out. She was running, the pavement uneven under her feet, and the street warped around her, hostile in its envelopment. She ran without knowing where she was going.

Sleep eluded her that night. The trio knew Mrs. Flanders personally and were taking up residence in her house now, maybe permanently. Could she still go there herself? Did Patrick know about them? He hardly seemed to notice her; Daisy doubted he could be any less vigilant than if they had stormed the house in front of him. Maybe they only came when he was gone, as she did, and that was why no one had ever thought to warn Daisy of them.

Before falling asleep, Daisy was struck by a wild panic. She reached into her backpack and realized the only thing she'd managed to pilfer from Mrs. Flanders' cabinets was a bag of chips, a roll of crackers, and a half-eaten jar of peanut butter. It would have to do, she told herself grimly. She'd gotten distracted and forgotten herself; she would go hungry as a consequence.

There was a jar of forgotten grape jelly and a pair of tuna cans. Somewhere in the silverware drawer were a few condiment packets from past takeout ventures. The last time she'd grabbed blindly from the Flanders kitchen, she'd gotten a family-size canister of pink lemonade mix. It was a sad parody of a feast, and the ensuing desperation emboldened her. She would wait it out for a day or two and go back like she'd planned. When she did, she would ask Mrs. Flanders if she was hosting any other kids.

"Was she?"

"What?"

"Was Mrs. Flanders hosting those kids you saw?"

"I don't really know if 'hosting' is what you'd call it. And anyways, I wasn't over there at night a lot."

"Never?"

"I didn't sleep over in that house, no. Tried not to, at least."

"Why not?"

"It was—there wasn't enough room."

"Not enough room."

"No."

"Well, when did you start hanging around with these three particular kids?"

"It's just that—one night at the house." She let out a long sigh. "I spent the night at Mrs. Flanders's house once. Only once."

Open House was tomorrow night, and Daisy needed a shower and a clean change of clothes. There was a dress, blue, with full sleeves and a floral pattern down the front; the flowers were daisies and she hated daisies, but it was her only dress, and it had been a gift. She would have help getting clean clothes. Ruth had known it was her sneaking clothes into the hampers and told her to drop the false pretenses: "You need clean clothes, I need clean clothes. You put the clothes in and let me go my way."

They had started Mrs. Flanders on new pain medication that made her even more of a mannequin than before. Assuming no one else was in the house, she could take her time in a shower, heat up some of the leftovers Ruth had left behind and have the television all to herself for the evening.

Her mother had promised to be in town in time to accompany her to meet her teachers. Freshman year and joining high school—surely her mother could grasp the significance of that. They had talked about going to dinner afterward once before, and it had since become a staple of their talks on the phone. Maybe she believed that reminding Daisy of her promises would foster the hope Daisy had of her actually acting on them; the truth was that the summer was half-dead, and not only had their temporary arrangement become the foundation of their newly distant relationship, but Daisy no longer asked about Nana and her suffering. She didn't ask about the home staff or about the new house they were going to get, and she didn't ask her mother to come home.

The girl with the red hair was called Avia. Daisy had described her to Mrs. Flanders; sweet, simple-minded, doped-up Mrs. Flanders, who nodded and smiled, even when no one said anything, and swayed in her seat, but that was the only person she could ask. Daisy tried to call up details that would clear the fog and was at a loss to push harder when comprehension didn't reveal itself in the old woman's face. "She was here the other day," Daisy tried to clarify, but Mrs. Flanders mistook her meaning.

"You're welcome anytime, dear. How is the school coming?" And Daisy was forced again to note the tremor in Mrs. Flanders's limbs and the translucent glow of her veined skin. Daisy had to let the matter go.

But she knew now that the girl was in the Flanders house from time to time and would probably continue to be so. She knew it was an inevitability that they would meet again, and she was right. The next day, she'd gotten up early enough to meet Ruth as she concluded her weekly regimen—to ask her to wash her dress and to see what she'd be leaving in the fridge—and there was the girl again, sitting next to a doddering Mrs. Flanders with her sightless eyes. Daisy expected the girl to look at her again with a cigarette and a snarl, but the girl was not concerned with Daisy. The girl's eyes—her expression indecipherable—were trained on Ruth's movements at the sink.

Daisy faltered in her footsteps, and the girl's gaze flashed to Daisy as she sat down gingerly at the table. She was hungry and needed clean clothes. Ruth had already given her permission to drop clothes off and, no matter what, she was not a coward. At this point, she was practically an adult, same as this girl whose gaze set Daisy's skin to crawl.

"Haven't seen you in a while." The girl's tone was laced with something verging on amusement. Daisy looked at her evenly and didn't respond. "You should've introduced yourself while you were here the other night while the boys were here. Could've sat down with us."

Daisy didn't respond. The girl searched her expression briefly and smiled at what she found. Her teeth were yellowed and chipped. Beside her, Mrs. Flanders trembled, and her clothes fluttered around her. The girl saw Daisy looking and nodded, as if to answer a question. "Yes, she's all messed up, isn't she? Shakes like she's on drugs. And really, she's on enough pain killers that she can't feel anything anymore. Doesn't know where she is either. Not really. Isn't that right, Auntie F?" She leaned over until her face hovered directly before the old woman's. "You have no clue what's going on."

Mrs. Flanders focused on her slowly. When understanding bloomed, her hands clasped the girl's cheeks tremulously.

"Avia! My sweet girl. Are you home from school?" Mrs. Flanders seemed seized by joy.

Avia smiled mechanically. A valiant struggle raged and was quickly smothered. Daisy felt weighted down in her seat, held still by a thousand invisible strings.

Avia wrested her face from Mrs. Flanders's grip and clasped the old woman's hands. "I don't go to school anymore, Auntie. Remember? I got out." To Daisy she said, "She has a hard time remembering."

Ruth was cutting fruit methodically and sliding the pieces off the knife into a large Tupperware bowl. Without looking at her, Avia said, "At least we have a maid, right? No, sorry—they're called therapists, excuse me. Pretty important work, isn't it." She leaned toward Daisy as if they were sharing a secret. "Putting an old lady in a chair and bending her legs and mashing her food to a pulp so she won't choke. Not enough people around in the States to do *that* kind of back-breaking work. Thank God for outsourcing, for sure." Throughout her speech Ruth did not turn or address them. She exited the kitchen without looking back, and they heard her slowly ascend the stairs. Avia turned her attention back to Daisy.

"So. What's your situation?"

Daisy spoke carefully. "My situation?"

"Your story. You aren't related to us, and you're not old or dirty enough to be one of Patrick's whores. That means there's something going on that's bringing you here."

There were fresh bananas and strawberries in the fruit bowl Ruth had abandoned. Daisy's stomach rolled in her frame. "My mother's out of town, and Mrs. Flanders lets me come here and crash so I don't go off by myself."

"Why is your mother gone?"

"She's…" The truth was no good. "She's working out of town."

"When will she come back?"

"I'm not sure. It's not the same every time."

Avia watched her and then nodded, accepting her answer. Abruptly, she got up and approached Daisy around the table. Gripping her arm in one hand, Avia yanked Daisy out of her seat and they moved toward the staircase.

There were three bedrooms on the second floor of the Flanders house. One was Mrs. Flanders's, one was Patrick's—still decorated the same as when he was in high school—and one was a dumping ground for all the junk a lifetime of carelessness could accumulate. Avia went to this one, budging the door open with some difficulty, Daisy lagging behind her. Daisy had seen the inside of the room once before and found it was no different; only a few more lungfuls of dust clogged her throat than last time.

"As you can see, this room is a total shithole. Auntie F told me you'd been staying with us the entire time, but, as you well know, Auntie F's brains have gone to hell." Avia kicked boxes out of her path until she came to a large dusted dresser on the opposite side of the room. "Most of the stuff in here was all my uncle's stuff anyway. She won't know if we throw it away. And even if she finds out, she'll forget." Avia turned back to look at Daisy, who had not moved beyond the doorway. "It'll probably take you all day to get it decent. I'll see if I can get a pizza here by eight."

Daisy weighed in on the situation. "I have a house with my mom. I stay there at night and come over during the day."

Daisy watched it come over Avia's face. It started at the crown of her forehead and drew in tight at her lips. Avia's expression was a dark blossom born of Daisy's recalcitrance. She took it back in the next breath, and Avia left her without another word.

It took her a few hours, but eventually there was a cot and a set of clean sheets that fit. The dresser had two drawers that still had knobs, and most of the boxes she opened were wattled with paper and broken remnants of a once-better life. By the time Avia came back with the pizza, Daisy had cleared a path around the furniture and divested the room of all the dead spiders she could find. The rooms were drafty on the second floor, and they ate side by side on the cot, eating quietly and efficiently with their hands.

"So you're staying here tonight." It wasn't a question.

Daisy nodded and swallowed. "Where will you sleep?" she asked, and Avia shrugged it off. She said she had a place lined up and that was all. Eventually, Daisy stood and resumed her work while Avia looked on, tilting her face to different parts of the clutter until Daisy descended upon it. They didn't trade small talk.

At some point, Avia made a show of wiping her hands on her sweatpants. "Okay, then. See you later." She walked to the door, and over Daisy's shoulder she heard Avia. "Make sure you keep the door closed tonight. And if you hear Auntie F calling, ignore it. Answering her only makes it worse."

Daisy listened to her thump down the staircase as she considered Avia's words. The cold air would circulate in the room if the door were left open, she reasoned, and besides, a closed door would give her more privacy. She put the matter out of her head and fell asleep quickly.

She slept more deeply than she had in weeks past. Perhaps that was why her reactions were delayed so long as the doorknob rattled and then wrenched in to turn and render the door open. Footsteps approached her, and a hot weight sank down near her left side. Her eyes opened blearily in the dark as she registered, dimwitted and too late, that a calloused hand rested on her naked thigh.

"This isn't…I don't really want to talk about this."

"Who was the person in your room, Daisy?"

"It wasn't my room. Remember? Not my house."

"Who was it?"

She paused. "Patrick."

"What did he do?"

"For a little bit, he didn't do anything. Just sat there next to me on the bed. Then he pulled the covers back and put his other hand on my other leg. That's when I stopped him."

"How did you stop him?"

"I just kind of sat up and he kind of froze. I think he thought I was still asleep."

"What happened next?"

"He just sat there for a long time. I kicked his hands off, and he moved back a little. I think he was drunk, because he kept rocking back and forth a little. After a while I just told him to go away."

"Did he say anything to you?"

"He told me…he told me I was beautiful. That he was here for me if I ever needed anything and that he considered us to be good friends now, since I was coming over to the house so much." Another pause. "I didn't even know he'd noticed me until then."

"Were you really spending all that time over there with him around? And you didn't think he would notice you?"

She gave a deep sigh. "Patrick's head is full of shit, Officer."

"Well, this guy was muffed up enough to assault you again." He tapped his pen. "Has he ever shown up at your house before? Maybe at your school?"

She shook her head no.

"Well, do you want to press charges? Make a statement?"

She paused, then shook her head no again.

"Why not, Daisy?"

She gave a shoulder shrug.

"You can't let him get away with everything he's done to you. Honestly, we've sent men like him away for less than this."

"He didn't even do anything that bad."

There was a new figure in the doorway. Shorter in stature and wider in the hips. Red hair glinting strangely in the dull hallway light.

Daisy didn't know why she hadn't bolted out of the house. As soon as he—that rat bastard—leaned in closer, she wrenched her leg back. She kicked him hard as she could in his chest and knocked him from his perch on the bed. They stared at each other, and then Patrick slowly rose from the floor.

"Well, then." He cocked his head at her.

He was waiting for some kind of response from her; an apology, maybe, or some kind of half-hearted assurance that everything was all right between them, that all was not lost. She stayed frozen, still halfway out of bed, as Patrick finally stumbled out of the bedroom and down the hall.

The sound of him died away, but the smell lingered. Daisy's breath began steadying in painful, tense increments and was still steadying as Avia appeared. She approached Daisy and stopped at the foot of the bed.

"He came in," she said, and Daisy nodded. Avia cleared her throat and reached suddenly to turn on the lamp placed on the floor near the cot. Daisy made an attempt to block her arm and failed; when the light came on, Avia didn't back off, but instead leaned over Daisy, studying her face. Daisy shrank back.

"Did he touch you?" After a moment Daisy nodded hesitantly. Avia nodded once. "Well, I doubt you'll be going back to sleep anytime soon, then." Avia grasped the edge of the blanket still hovering over Daisy's lap and cleanly tore it loose. "Will you? Sufficiently freaked out, are you?" She chuckled grimly. "Well, then, come on. You'll hang with me tonight." She headed to the door, indifferent to Daisy's reticence. "Throw on some clothes and come downstairs. Sun's almost up."

It was not Daisy that rose from the bed, but someone else. When she stood from the cot, not-Daisy pulled on the pants and jacket she'd worn the day before. She came downstairs to find Avia looking out the window into the front yard. She shuffled from foot to foot expectantly.

As the morning light cracked through the heavy curtain of night, they heard a car coming down the street. It signaled its arrival with blaring music which rose to a deafening roar as it parked in the driveway. The driver honked once in the driveway without turning the engine off. Avia waved once to the car from the window, and when Daisy approached she looked over Avia's shoulder.

It was the two boys she'd seen under the lamp that night, the same two who'd sandwiched Avia on the couch the night Daisy snuck in.

Avia ran a hand through her hair, attempting to smooth it into place. She darted around Daisy and ran to the bathroom, and Daisy listened to her run water from the sink. When she returned Avia strode to the door, jerking toward it with her chin at Daisy as she made to unjam the lock. "Let's go."

"I don't want to."

Avia's hands slowed as they twisted and jingled the bolt. She faced the door as she spoke. "Oh, yeah?"

"I don't think it's a good idea."

"Then what is a good idea?" Avia turned the lock and pulled the door open. She turned to Daisy with her back to the outside. "You going to stay here and have it out with dear, darling Patrick? Let him make you breakfast and put his hand up your shirt? You think there's something for you here?" She stared hard at Daisy, and when Daisy wouldn't answer, said, "At least with us you'll get some food—and get out of the house. You aren't doing that, you aren't doing anything. You sure as hell don't have nobody waiting around for you." With that, she walked out the door, a brusque "hurry your ass up" as she stomped down the lawn.

The sun would be up in a couple hours. She had watched Mrs. Flanders make a pathetic attempt at descending the stairs once at the beginning of the summer and didn't want to see it again. And in the meantime, there was stale, unappealing food in the Flanders pantry and rotting food in hers.

Daisy turned her head away from the window and the car, still parked and alive with music. She thought about grabbing another jacket and then realized she wouldn't know where to even look for one. She caught a glimpse of herself in the reflection of the window glass and couldn't stop looking at her eyes, wide and shocked. She wasn't speaking, and her mouth was closed as though sewn shut. Without giving herself another moment to think, she hurried to the door and let herself out.

She didn't look back.

"Did you end up going?"

"Where—Open House Night?"

"Yes."

"Yes." She shrugged her shoulders. "Yes. Avia took me."

"Oh, yeah? How did that work out?"

"She said she was my sister. Kind of gave the teachers a hard time." She let out a soft snort. "It was funny, actually."

"I bet."

Avia walked her home from school that night, and for those few blocks neither spoke.

Daisy had been surprised even before they set foot on her school campus. Before attending Open House Night, they had gone to eat at the Waffle House: she, Avia, and the stone-faced boys, Tommy and Jesus. Daisy split a plate of pancakes with Avia with hash browns and scrambled eggs, and Avia let Daisy take the lion's share of the food. For her part, Avia was too busy wielding a cigarette like a baton and dumping ashes every time she wanted to punctuate the statement she made. The waitress was not shy in her disgust at the smoke—but Daisy was astounded and intoxicated by her brazenness.

She learned later to think of spending time with Avia like she was spending time with a wild animal in its natural habitat. Under Avia's tutelage, everything had to be relearned. The streets of Pleasant Valley, once so ordinary and certain, became a new world through the lens of Avia's eyes, and Daisy struggled to decipher the masses of sensations and signals that bombarded her at every second during their time together.

Her mother did not make it in time to take her to Open House. The most surprising part was that she actually called Daisy in time to tell her. "When the school year starts I'll come by the school and introduce myself," she said, and Daisy listened to the traffic in the background as she watched cars pass her from where she sat. "They'll let me do that later on, don't you think? And don't you think that'll be more personal than just showing up with all the other parents?"

After she hung up, Daisy turned and saw Avia watching her. Blessedly, she said nothing, and the meal was paid for and they left. The boys dropped her and Avia off far enough into the valley to walk home and then slunk off. Upon getting her to the curb of her house, Avia left Daisy with, "I'll be here at seven." Then she turned and walked off.

Daisy let herself into the dark house and lay in her bed without falling asleep. The unfamiliar sensation of a full stomach gave her a buzz of physical contentedness but did nothing to quell her churning thoughts. She didn't want to go to her teachers without a parent, and she didn't want to lie abandoned in the house all night. She hadn't wanted to leave the diner and hadn't wanted to go eat at all. She wanted everything and had *nothing* and knew that both were essentially the same.

She had a new group of people to spend time with, though. That was something. People to fill the silent moments and hold a conversation with her; people to spend time with her and give her something to do with her hands, her limbs, her words. Maybe when she was stuck in class or out walking the blocks or watching the sun set over the rolling hills, she could think on Avia and the boys and feel like she had someone in her life. Her mother used to play that role, but lately she had been stalling for more and more time away. Daisy hardly expected to see her anymore. But this girl with red hair and jagged teeth was different. Avia said she would be back, and Daisy had to believe that she would. She was surprised at herself, though. A small ball of anticipation lay in her stomach. She *wanted* Avia to come back. She lay on her bed and thought: Seven will get here in no time at all. Then we can go out. The thought warmed her into closing her eyes and drifting off.

A knock broke her reverie. She must have slipped into the ether, because the noise echoed in her ears. The knocking tapered off; Daisy heard nothing. Then a hand with short hot fingers was shaking her awake. "I told you to be ready for me," Avia's voice said.

Daisy rolled over and sat up. She moved to face Avia, who filled every corner of the room, standing only at the foot of Daisy's bed. "Can probably brush out your hair and get the knots out and no one will know. I would pull your bangs over those lines on your forehead, though. You've got some serious creases going on." Avia swept a pair of pants aside with her foot and sat down on the floor near Daisy's closet. "Let's go. Chop-chop."

Daisy felt the tendrils of a tantrum unfurling and marveled at herself. Who was this girl, this rebellious, foul-mouthed outcast who flashed a tattooed wrist from under the sleeve of her hoodie and leaned in too close when she spoke? This girl who had somehow appointed herself Daisy's new caretaker and got aggressive when she resisted?

"What time does this thing start, anyway? Eight? Nine?"

"Why do you even care?" Daisy turned her head and fixed Avia with a stare that she hoped was severe. "What does it matter to you?"

Avia met the gaze evenly and did not laugh, breaking the look after a moment only to play with the fringe of her shirt and brush her hair out of her eyes. "I've seen you around, you know. Seen your mom going to and from. Used to see you walking on your own—going to school, I guess, or to sell scrap. Noticed you were always alone."

And what to say to that? "Yes," Daisy said, and felt hollow. "So I'm alone a lot. So what."

"The thing is," Avia continued casually, ignoring Daisy, "I'm not the only one who sees you. This is a dangerous neighborhood. Safety comes in numbers, you know that. People know your mom's flown and that you don't have nobody else. People who might be looking to take advantage. Surprised you haven't been 'visited' already, tell you the truth. You need someone. Someone looking after you." Avia lifted her chin. "That's why I'm here."

Avia got up and walked to Daisy's bedroom door. "Give you ten minutes." She strolled out. Daisy heard her feeling her way to the living room and curse at something she found. Daisy climbed slowly out of bed, feeling old and spent, and stuffed her feet back into her sneakers. There was an old sweater hanging off her closet door; she grabbed it and wrapped it around herself, not looking at her reflection in the mirror. She crept down the hallway and stood behind the couch to find Avia waiting.

Avia turned to look at her appraisingly. A slow, easy smile arose on her face, her jagged teeth displayed prominently. "All right," she said. "Let's go."

SEPTEMBER

ON THE FIRST DAY OF the month, Daisy awoke face down in her bed. It was Saturday. The night before, Daisy had been eating a bologna sandwich by candlelight when Avia appeared. "We're going scrapping." And for four hours they drove across the valley, playing Led Zeppelin softly and revving the car in the neighborhoods—she, Avia, and the two boys, Jesus and Tommy.

The system was simple: trawling down the bumpy roads looking for junked cars and other promising piles. Jesus would usually drive, and Tommy sat beside him, smoking and staring out the window, muttering to himself all the while. Avia and Daisy were tasked with holding flashlights out the backseat windows and watching out for potential hits; every mile or so, Avia would flag down a junker and declare that it was "definitely worth the gamble, oh yeah, definitely. The outside ain't the important part anyways, is it?" If the boys approved, they would shift gears, cut the lights, and dart out together.

They always worked in the dead of night. Sometimes they would hear voices and cut off curses and angry rumblings, and Avia kept Daisy close while they waited, a hand clutching her shoulder, her neck—fingers combing through her disheveled hair. Sometimes Avia spent the time alone telling Daisy dirty jokes to get her to smile or spun rags out of the roundabouts of her young life.

"Hey," Avia said mischievously once, waiting for Daisy to look over. When she did, Avia asked, "What did the blind man say to the fish stand when he passed it?" Avia waited, then: "Good morning, ladies!"

And later: "I watched a guy die once," she told Daisy. "I saw my house burn down to the ground. Both times, I had my sister with me. I was pushed and pushed and pushed, and I did a lot of terrible shit. But you know, you have good times with the bad, always. Like, okay, my mom used to make us Fox in the Hole, right? It's like a hot dog that's been baked in the bread. We would eat that and watch Disney movies together, make a fort in the living room. And, like, prom and hanging out with your friends. There's a lot of sad stuff, out here like this, but there are good things too."

The trunk of the car was busted and fastened closed with fishing wire, and the boys would deposit their scores, slipping back into their seats as if they'd never left. They were old hands at it now, Avia said, and the business was smooth and easy—most nights. "Every now and again we get a spotter, but that's no problem. It's nothing to stick the throttle and just *go*." She made a sweeping motion with her hand to encompass a swift flight. "I'm telling you, easiest money you could ever get out here. Much better than the trade too; seems like nowadays all anybody wants is a pill or a blunt, but the fuzz'll snuff you for that shit right quick. No one is going to check out on some little scrap deal. No point to it."

"But it's still totally illegal," Daisy said. Avia snorted ruefully.

"Yeah? Just about everything is now, I guess. But we ain't killing no one, and we ain't hurting nothing. And really," she said decisively, "survival itself ain't illegal. We're just trying to make it out here."

After a successful run, they would go down to Jung's and cash in their wares. Jesus was always impatient to get paid; he would rush down the narrow road, bumping and thumping and stampeding, blasting the music freely then skid right up to the rickety gate and honk the horn twice. He and Tommy would haul everything in while Jung watched from the halo of light his porch light cast, arms crossed like a disapproving father. Sometimes they went inside Jung's office-house—to haggle or guarantee their pay was fair, Avia said. They usually came back after an hour or so, sometimes longer; occasionally the thin curtains would betray the shadows cast by movement, and Daisy would watch Jung wave his arms and jab forward, pull back as the boys hemmed him in, never out of step with one another.

Jesus and Tommy would stroll out without a goodbye and the gate could never seem to close quickly enough behind them. Then they would then head for the boulevard and eat their earnings. "Shame to have to work if you can't eat," Avia had said the night before as she handed Daisy a sandwich. They had managed to catch The Burger Barrel just in time before they closed.

Daisy rolled onto her back and blew the hair out of her face. It was her mother, home again, rattling around in the kitchen and opening up every cupboard to discover their emptiness, she knew. The slamming doors sounded like distant gongs and echoed in every crevice of the empty house. It had been some time since her mother had gotten home early enough to wake her, and if she knew her mother at all, she would be bounding into Daisy's room next—trying, with a falsetto voice and a handful of tired clichés to make it more of a reunion than a chance meeting.

She wasn't wrong. "Daisy, my *darling*," her mother sang as she nudged the door open and waved her arms in a flourish. "I hoped I would find you still asleep. Remember when you were little and I would gather you in my arms and rock you awake? Of course," her mother said, scrunching her nose playfully, "you were little and willing back then. Not so sure I could get away with that now."

Daisy sat up just in time to receive her mother's hug. With her face jammed into the crook of her neck, she became aware of the smell of cigarettes and the thin scent of cheap perfume layered over it. Her mother was unwashed, unkempt, and felt swollen in her arms. A sudden feeling of loss overcame Daisy, and she gripped her mother in a spasm. This was her *mother*, her mother dear, her special friend, who lit candles with special names and grabbed her arms to dance with her in the kitchen. They stayed locked together, and the moment seemed to stretch on, tense and quiet.

"I really have missed you, lamb chop." The words were muffled by hair.

Daisy wanted to respond in kind. She wanted to describe all the past horrors she had endured and the dread that bedeviled her. The nights and days spent alone; the cold, persistent and inescapable in the new fall; the moments that drew Daisy to Avia. She wanted to address the gaping maw of the chasm she saw every time she looked at her mother's face, but as she corralled herself to say the words, she heard, "On another note, your room is so cluttered, chickadee. When was the last time you did laundry?" And in the next instant she was peeling herself away and trying to adopt an expression that said nothing had changed; not the house, the distance, her.

"It's been a while," she finally said, and tried to heft some humor into it. "Been quite a while."

"She came home that week to tell me Nana had died."

"She died in the nursing home?"

"Yeah. They had the funeral in Halbart, so Mom came and got me. Not a lot of people showed up."

"Why didn't you stay with your mother the rest of the summer? Or why didn't your mother come back to town after that? The whole reason she was gone was to care for your nana, right?"

"Well, yeah, but that wasn't all of it." She leaned forward. "I figured that, too, that she would come back as soon as Nana died. But Nana didn't have all of her stuff together when she got sick, and then when she died all of it was just kind of up in the air. Mom said Nana had some money left over from a fund or whatever, and that there was a life insurance account. Somebody at the home was giving her the numbers and papers she needed to get the money. She talked about getting a lawyer for a while."

"And so she was just…what? Waiting around to get a settlement?"

"Yeah, basically. Well, and she'd gotten a job at the home. Spent so much time there, eventually they just gave her a cleaning job." She paused. "That's where she was getting the money for the bills. The bills we paid, at least."

"So why not at least go stay with her in Halbart in the meantime?"

"Because she wanted to keep our house." She nodded as his eyebrows shot up. "No, seriously, that's what she said. I know, I know, the house—you've seen it, right?—the house is a total dump, but it's the only one Mom's ever had of her own, and it's the only one I can remember." She let out a huff of a laugh. "Could live anywhere and it wouldn't change anything."

"What do you mean by that?"

Another pause. "Nothing."

"Fine. Did you at least tell your mother about this situation you had with these kids? What's her name again—Avina?"

"Avia. And, no, I didn't. When she would ask, I would say that things were going okay with Mrs. Flanders and that I wasn't lonely or anything. That's all she ever really wanted to hear anyway."

"But then Mrs. Flanders fell."

"Yeah." She let out a longer sigh this time, and it was awhile before she spoke again. "Yeah, she did."

Her jeans were clean and snug, her belly was full from leftovers, and as she walked down the block clad in a new hoodie—left in her room for her to find, folded on her bed with the tag still attached—Daisy found herself humming a tune she didn't recognize. She stopped as the Flanders house came into view from the end of the street.

Her nana was dead. During the funeral, laid out stiffly in her coffin, Daisy had only been able to stare blankly at the body and try to remember what the old woman had been like in the parts of her life Daisy was present for. Few as those moments were, Daisy recalled that her nana's apartment—a nice setup, despite the neighbors and the noise—always smelled like cats and baby powder. That was during those last few years before the home, but her body still trembled, and she still blanked out mid-sentence sometimes. Daisy's mother kept their visits short but always had good things to say about the woman who raised her.

"My mother? Useless, totally useless. Nana, though, she was so good to me, forever."

Perhaps it was that sentiment that inspired her mother to drop everything and fly to Halbart when she'd gotten the call months back. Still, she didn't cry or convulse as the casket was lowered, and neither did Daisy. They ate at a buffet after the service, and her mother hummed and beamed and giggled. She nudged Daisy's arms and ruffled her hair, carrying on like they were at a Sunday dinner. She said that soon, everything was going to change. "Nana always did right by me," her mother gushed. "Always. And she's going to help us get out of the slump we've been in so long." There was some money tied up in Nana's name, and if she could get all the forms in one time, it could be a sizable sum.

"I knew there had to be some stack put away that was paying the home off all these years, but I wasn't going to ask her, just wanted the best for her. But the money that's left has to go somewhere, and I'm the next of kin. So-ooo-o," her mother drew the vowel out, "I'm thinking as soon as we get everything filed, we'll pay off the house. Pay off the car—hell, we'll get a *new* car! We've always wanted to go to Disneyland. How about this summer? And I'm going to come home." She took Daisy's hand across the table. "And you have been so good for me this summer, holding it down out here for me, I'm going to make it all up to you." She squeezed Daisy's hand and returned to her own plate.

Of course, nothing was guaranteed, not yet. There was a small mountain of paperwork to be done, and maybe even a civil suit to be built; there would be fees to pay in order to get this and that, and sometimes there were fees just to move the process along. In the meantime, Daisy's mother had a good setup at the nursing home and was going to stay.

"Four nights a week there, and I'll be here for the rest of it. And that'll only be until we get this all sorted out. Then everything'll get better." But even if they couldn't get better, Daisy would settle for things going back the way they were before. And as she walked that night, let herself in the gate and fished out her key, she felt a twinge of some cousin to contentment grace her heart. She wondered how she would break the news to Avia, or if she even would. Avia would probably say that it was about damn time Daisy's mother made an effort to show up.

"Ghost parents only work in the sitcoms, Daisy darling. Haven't I taught you anything?"

Avia was always trying to teach Daisy things: how to sneak into movie theaters and only miss the opening trailers; how to make a casserole with the bare essentials; how to smoke cigarettes without getting hooked on the nicotine, which Daisy failed at; and how to hotwire a car, which Daisy mastered within a week. Every moment spent with Avia was a long, unending tutorial, and Daisy never forgot a thing.

Most of the conversations she and Avia had consisted of Avia trying to convince Daisy of all the things she shouldn't be or do in life: She shouldn't leave a job before securing another one, but she would never fool herself into believing that a job will last forever. She shouldn't allow herself to be bartered or sold, but she should always remember that everything, down to her body itself, *could* be sold for the right price. And above all, loyalty was the agreement, terms and contract that governed an average life, and whatever or whomever Daisy gave her loyalty to would play a role in all of her important life decisions. It would bind her to people, places, things. It would be her only real choice in life and give birth to a thousand other little choices, becoming the grains of sand that formed the shoreline of her destiny.

She used that word—destiny—like she was handing it to Daisy herself.

Eventually, her loyalties would make the decisions for her. And loyalty, like any other thing worth having, was worth investing. But what deserved her loyalty most?

"Some people might say family, others might say a job, getting up just to work just to lie back down. And other people put their loyalty to a church or a building—for the symbol of it, you know, the *prestige*—and some helpless fools say their loyalty is safest with the government. There's only one place to put your loyalty and know for sure it's safe."

They were sitting on the steps of the Flanders's backyard porch, surrounded by dirt and the bone scraps left over from a dog that lived there once. Avia, having finished her speech, leaned into the smoke of her cigarette and seemed to ignore Daisy, who understood the game by then and waited for the punch line. "The *self*." Avia's lips curled strangely around the words, as if she'd only just acquired them. "Put all you got—hope, love, faith, allegiance, all of it—in yourself. How much more of a guarantee can you ask for?" And she dumped her ashes in salute.

Avia talked big, with big gestures. She spoke like someone who had stolen the secrets of the universe somehow and was selling them for far less than they were worth, and Daisy was her only audience—her pupil, her star prodigy. She said she'd had a sister once, and a mother before that, and both were gone. She said she and the brothers she ran with now were her family, but it wasn't a family—merely animals who recognized each other's species. She said the world was heartless and desolate, but Daisy was smart and still good, "Not all used up and dry, like me." Daisy could reach out and still seize the heart of life, hold it beating in her hands and *own* it, and Avia promised that she would show her how. "And maybe one day…who knows, you'll return the favor to me. But for now, we have to take our living as we can get it and do as we see fit."

Conversations that veered into the abstract were the closest thing to a challenge that could be met at two in the morning, sitting on a rotting porch step. Daisy tilted her head, considered this a moment, and then offered her rebuttal: "So, no family or friends? It's totally wrong to be loyal to anyone else? What happens if you ever get caught in a jam and need help to get out?"

Avia snorted and refolded her legs. "Why do you think you end up in jams? Who do you think causes problems in your life? And can you always trust that those people will stick with you?" She chuckled and dragged on her cigarette. "Me, myself and I: Make that your new mantra."

They left the subject at that.

If Daisy had asked, she would have wondered why Avia insisted on such an isolationist outlook, and then defied it by always glancing prospectively at the sullen boy who seemed to be her partner in everything she did. Avia said that Jesus was tied down and burdened with family problems, but he came at her whim and heeded her signals. For her part, too, Avia seemed to be tethered to him, and when they walked, they walked side by side, not holding hands or clasped at the hips, but leaning toward each other, measuring their steps and matching the other's stride. It was a joining that appeared seamless.

Daisy approached the door with gusto and was surprised to find it unlocked. From the archway, she heard the television blaring in the living room. The jingle to a popular insurance commercial chimed from within. Avia and the boys would be inside.

She strode into the room to find it desolate and abandoned.

She started, turned halfway back to the front door, repositioned to face the window. Hadn't the boys' car been parked in the drive earlier? Had they mentioned any errands she'd forgotten from the night before? The driveway was empty. She let the curtain fall back and, turning, saw the living room with new eyes; the sofa was turned out of its usual place, and the coffee table was littered with trash. Someone had eaten a full plate of food and left the dishware there, and the lamp set against the wall tilted precariously in its stand, wires protruding. It had been knocked over at some point. There was the stench of grease and something rotten suddenly; the television was turned up way too loud.

Under that haze of noise was a pervading depth, and Daisy was slapped with the realization that the entire house had been ransacked, instantly and resolutely.

Too slowly did she hear the hoarse cries. Too slowly did she hear rattling, rustling noises, faint and brief, somewhere in the dank upper lifts of the house. Too slowly, too *lethargically* her limbs moved as she made her way up the stairs. And as she reached the top stair, too quickly did she pause and turn back, snapping her neck back so hard the tendons jerked, turning quickly back to look back at the living room, and behind that, the kitchen. The back door slammed as she neared the second floor, and she screamed.

The lights were on in Mrs. Flanders's room and her room alone. The light pooled the hallway floor, the door left slightly ajar like an invitation. Daisy hesitated before stepping inside. The sparse room had been violated. The sheets torn haphazardly from the bed, the knickknacks knocked off the shelves. When she rounded the bed and found the crumpled wisp of a woman sprawled across the carpet, Daisy recognized the dark matter unfurled beneath Mrs. Flanders's head. It seeped into the soles of her shoes at the same pace as her infringing terror.

Somewhere in the darkness, a figure was moving stealthily away from the horror they'd wrought against a poor old woman in a derelict old house. And somewhere, too, was a black junker gliding gracelessly down the block, blaring music and looking lively as ever as it ambled home. But Daisy was there, leaning against the wall of that bedroom wishing she were somewhere, anywhere else in the world. For her, trembling and terrified, shamed into action, the call to the paramedics and the wait thereafter was a journey that seemed to have no end.

The easy banter of Avia and the boys coming home just in time to beat the screaming sirens was snuffed out as soon as flashing lights shone on the sides of the house. Daisy crept to the spare bedroom and watched the front yard from the window. No one in the junker moved at first—even Jesus let the car slide down the driveway in reverse until he braked. Avia beat everyone else inside.

From the top of the staircase, Daisy ran to meet her. Avia burst in the door and stopped at the sight of her. They looked at each other, and Avia searched her face. She seemed to be searching for something there. Daisy shuddered at the expressions that flashed on Avia's face.

Men stormed in with uniforms and equipment. They shoved past Avia, and Daisy scuttled a retreat to the bedroom that had once been hers. There were harsh, complex words sounding off like a firing squad through the wall. Something about a hemorrhage, "Oxygen, give her oxygen" and "No, no, brace it, here."

Later, after the men had left and the haze had lifted, Daisy ventured to creep out of the bedroom and paused again at the staircase. Avia was waiting, sitting on the bottom step. Daisy heeded the call, moving slowly, as if wounded, close enough to speak and wait. She waited what seemed like hours for Avia to finally talk, to ask her what happened and have Daisy make her defense. She found herself waiting longer still for Avia to forgive her.

It was an absolution that would not come for many nights.

"So what do you think happened to Mrs. Flanders?"

"I don't know, man." She pitched forward, holding her head in her hand, faintly whispering. "Even now I'm not so sure. For a while I was convinced I saw a man walking out the back door, and sometimes I think I saw her getting killed, but it's all just my imagination. Visions, I guess."

"Did you get blamed for what happened?"

"Yes. Well…yes and no. It wasn't my fault, but it was my responsibility."

"What do you mean?"

"If I'd gotten to the house sooner, Mrs. Flanders might not have been hurt. Or, maybe she would've been, but I would have seen who did it. So, it's like, I didn't hurt her, but I didn't protect her neither."

"Did the others start treating you differently?"

"Avia did, yeah. God, there were days she wouldn't even look at me."

"Did that change?"

"Yeah." She gave a grim laugh. "Took a lot, but yeah."

"What happened that changed it?"

"One day, clear out of the blue, she said the boys figured out who did it."

Daisy was wrapped in a dream. She was in a fog, and it swarmed her. It was in her clothes, in her hair—diving into her nose and mouth only to come pouring out of her ears. There were sparks of light—flashes of color and small bursts of sound—and she was floating, distended in ageless time and senseless place. She was light and easy for a time, but at the edges of her consciousness rose walls, erected quickly and closing in fast. They slammed into place the moment her eyes fluttered open, and she realized a pair of hands lay wrapped around her throat.

The biggest mistake she could make would be to move too quickly or fight back. She lay still as death and waited for the fingers to unclench. They did, but not without squeezing down one last time. She did not give in to fear and gasp for breath and focused on training her eyes directly above her.

The presence dipping the bed alongside her shifted back once and then forward again. "I seem to remember you feeling pretty torn up for the late, great Auntie F," the darkness said huskily. "Was wondering if you were finally ready to do something about it."

"She isn't dead yet," Daisy whispered. "Patrick visited her yesterday and said she was already doing better."

The bed shifted again; Avia lurched over her oppressively. "Is that what you really believe? Because you know that's bullshit, and you certainly ain't that stupid." Avia was sneering and Daisy cringed at the violence her tone promised. "Just for the fun of it, let me ask you again: remember anything else?"

It had been like this all week: the few times Avia deigned to talk to Daisy directly were brief and devoid of eye contact or touch. Before, Avia was always touching Daisy, putting a hand in her hair when they ordered fast food, grabbing her arm for support when they jumped a fence; leaning on her as they sat on the sofa and watched trash television while the boys smiled and elbowed each other. With the absence of touch came a domineering silence, only strengthened by the boys' continual indifference to Daisy. The unspoken blame was the final blow, draped over Daisy like a blanket and smothering her.

Avia had once explained to Daisy the difference between a fault and a responsibility. "When it's a fault, you done it, and you face up for it, one way or another. When it's a responsibility, it's given to you—whether you want it or not." Mrs. Flanders had been pushed down the fast track to the grave, and Avia held Daisy responsible for it.

"I don't know what happened, Avia," Daisy murmured to the ceiling. She spoke low and reverently. "Honest, I've told you everything already."

For the first time in days, Avia was looking at her—pinning her in place with a hard stare, and Daisy wondered what she saw on her face. Desperation, undoubtedly. "Well, then. You know I'll always give you the benefit of the doubt, Daisy darling. You know that, right?" Daisy nodded. The weight on the bed lifted smoothly. "Suppose you're ready to get a move on, then."

Gingerly, Daisy sat up. "Where are we going?" she asked. "Scrapping?" They'd made their worst haul yet two nights after Mrs. Flanders had been found.

Avia should her head. "No, no, we got to move fast on this if we want to have it our way. No time to go scrapping. Best to do it tonight." Avia made sure Daisy was watching as she strode over to Daisy's closet. "You got that one shirt I like clean? And the hoodie—the one I gave you, where is that?"

Daisy found the clothing requested and dressed. Avia ushered her out quickly, and to Daisy's surprise the boys were parked and waiting outside her house, the first time they'd ever done so. Avia rushed her into the car and into her seat, unusually pushy and feverishly excited. The boys were even more somber than usual. Daisy buckled her seatbelt with the sinking feeling that she'd signed away something intangible, and she clung to the belt strap as the car rolled away.

The drive was short and silent, pregnant with expectation. Daisy's mind was far afield, reeling in the backseat as the car dove into the sloping hills and burrows in the backdrop of their journey. The moon was bright, and the dry, brittle grass glowed like the filaments of so many gossamer strands of a spider's web, and on that night the grasses undulated with an eerie animation; Daisy tried only to focus on the street lamps that heralded the way. Any one of the trees and telephone poles they passed could've been the stranger that assaulted Mrs. Flanders, and Daisy searched the profiles of each feebly, looking for an answer that had slipped away.

Avia had a hand at the nape of her neck and clamped down as though Daisy would fling herself from the car at any moment. They came to their destination quickly enough, and any shadow of choice was gone. Daisy was surprised to recognize the house as they approached. They had scored from the property plenty of times.

She didn't want to get out of the car. No, she didn't want any part of what was about to happen. She looked down in a daze to see that her hands were still clinging to her seatbelt. Avia was leaning over her and undoing her buckle, then moving roughly over her to jump out the backseat, and then dragging her out a second later. She realized numbly they were meant to show their strength by appearing as a pack, and her knees nearly gave out. They had to half-drag, half-carry Daisy up to the black, crumbling shack, where drywall filled a massive wound in the front wall.

Jesus approached the door first. In the silence, his knock was like a strike to the body. Daisy prayed no one would answer, but a muffled curse and the noises of kicking and scuffling soon sounded, and then the door opened with a tilt—not fully wedded to the door hinge.

Someone gasped—like they had been gutted—as Bobby Jenkins stepped out of the door frame just enough to reveal his face. His expression was a scowl, and he was shirtless, clutching a rag in the hand that braced against the doorframe. Half-twisted, feet still planted inside the house, he canted his head to the side and waited for their cue, the only gesture he made that said he expected them.

Jesus spoke first. He said that there had been word that Bobby had been on their street the night Mrs. Flanders had been attacked. Sources they had on good authority said they definitely saw him cutting through their alley right before they came home that night. Bobby smiled coolly and guffawed, said he had no business around that block; and besides, "Where you getting these sources, kid? Because it sure as hell wasn't me."

Jesus said he guessed that Bobby knew they'd been swiping from his yard for parts for weeks, and if that was all that was between them, they could've settled it another way—paid him a cut or replaced parts or something. No need to crunch an old lady, Jesus said, reciting his words like he'd memorized them, and Bobby laughed again, a sick, wet-bag sound.

"Still ain't said I did it," Bobby chided, and waved his arm across him and them. "Got too much to do half the time, wasting my days on some small stones like that. Whose aunt was it, now? Because I can't even recollect." He leaned out too far to hover, and he swayed uncertainly. "Tell you what." He slung an arm around Jesus' shoulders. "The old bag kicks it, I'll send you a bouquet of flowers." Bobby pulled a giggle from somewhere inside himself. Pushing the fringe out of his eyes, Bobby leaned in close, chest to chest. "I'll buy you a field of flowers, you just tell me when. Hey, macho man?"

The first swing came too quick for Daisy to see it. In slow motion, Bobby's face began a series of transformations. He was blinking, stuttering, moving to stumble back, or perhaps even moving to block the attack. A flash of dull red hair blurred, and Avia was swinging, clubbing, jabbing and contacting with each blow. She struck him once, and the arm he'd put up was deflected. She struck him twice more, and he was on the ground. Daisy couldn't see Avia's face, but a feral sob hummed from her chest, punctuated by the blows. The sounds of dying, too, were thunderous, with Bobby making whining, wheezing, whimpering sounds. From outside herself, Daisy felt the cage of her chest and the stinging pricks in her vision as the oldest valley crook's face caved in a way that was wholly unnatural.

The boys pulled Daisy away eventually, uprooted her. Where had Avia gotten the bat? Daisy didn't know. She didn't know how they got off that cursed land, or if they left Bobby bleeding in his doorway. Maybe she vomited at one point, because the smell of it never left the clothes she wore that night, and she eventually threw them away. She woke up the next afternoon with her face in the pillow, just as she had so many times before. The mundanity of it enraged her, and she bit at her flesh like a rabid dog. She stayed in bed all day, wondering if the sight of bare bones and thin blood would ever stop appearing every time she closed her eyes.

"Daisy." His voice was gentle. "Why didn't you try to get help?"

Her head snapped up." Don't…don't you do that. Don't you touch me. You have no idea…what it was like."

"I understand your fear. You watched a man being killed before your eyes. It's a lot to take in, especially since it was so violent."

"It didn't bother anyone but me. The others didn't care. I bet—I bet they'd done it before. Had never seen Avia with the bat. Didn't even know she had it."

"And that's all you did? Just watch?" And then, seeing the change in her face, he said, "Daisy."

"She made me. She made me, she made me. She said I had to. She would've left me there. Cradling face; trembling hands, muffled voice. I didn't want to. Swear to Christ, I didn't want to."

"Did anything else happen that night? Anything at all?"

"I went—I wanted—I tried." She stuttered to a stop and took a huge gulp of air. Her breaths were slow and unsteady. "I didn't know what to do. I didn't know what was going to happen next. I did something stupid."

"And what is that?"

By the time the car rattled up to the curb outside her house, Daisy had sunk into some part of herself. Avia didn't hesitate: Daisy felt the car door at her side open, and impossibly gentle hands, feverish and calloused, were tugging her out of her seat, hefting under her arms and hauling her out, the rest of her dragging behind. Avia tried to be tender, humming as she carried Daisy to her bed. She peeled back the dirty sheets and set Daisy down awkwardly. Eventually, Daisy was swaddled, the comforter tucked right under her chin. When she was satisfied with her bundle, Avia sat at Daisy's side and leaned over her.

Daisy turned her head and looked with unseeing eyes. Avia's voice came from far away.

"You sleep here tonight. Don't be scared, and keep your head down. Check in with you soon." And then, softer still: "You did good tonight. Proud of you." She reached with blunt fingers and scratched down Daisy's hairline and quickly crept out. Daisy lay there, encased in the dark coffin of her body. Her thoughts rose and fell at the same pace as the shallow breaths rattling her flayed lungs.

When the wave finally crested, she blinked and came back to herself; she was standing outside a house that was not her own, her blanket still draped across her shoulders, dragging on the ground at her feet.

Sissy Tompkins's yard was especially laughable this time of year. Daisy felt crowded just standing on the fringe of the grass. Her mind was awash with static, and her body moved without her consent. Sissy's bedroom was on the left side of the house in the corner, a small window held closed by duct tape. Daisy ripped two bottom strips out and hissed for Sissy to come before she could stop herself.

After a time, half of Sissy's face slotted itself before the opening. She blinked uncomprehendingly several times before coming awake, and rasped, "What in *God's* name, D?" But the girls only stared at one another dumbly before Sissy muttered, "Wait here," and retreated back into the darkness. Eventually, Daisy heard the snap of the hinge on Sissy's back door, like gunfire in the dark, and then Sissy was taking her by the hand and leading her away from the house.

"Okay, girl," she said once they'd walked a respectable distance. "Let's hear it. All the kids who could've showed up here at the dead hour, and it's *you?*" She laughed warmly. "Must be something good."

She must have thought Daisy was going to curse and cry and tell her that she'd fought with her mother and been kicked out of the house. Maybe Daisy was pregnant and needed help preparing to face her mother. Or maybe Daisy was in love with Sissy, as Sissy claimed two sophomores had been last semester, and thought the moonlight and spontaneity of it all would help her case. But Daisy stuttered that a man had been killed, and she had helped; that he had bled out, and that Daisy had touched the blood. That it was all over now, the remains were taken care of—but she just couldn't sleep.

When she finished, Daisy looked at Sissy through her hair and tried to discern her expression. She was so still and quiet that Daisy could have almost mistaken her for an illusion.

"You are so full of shit, Young," Sissy finally said.

She had never used Daisy's last name before. She didn't sound like herself. She turned and walked slowly back to her house, as if hacking through thick foliage, not bothering to be as quiet as Daisy would have been.

Daisy waited pointlessly for something to happen. She knew it was a blind, foolish hope she'd held—that saying the words out loud would change things. Nothing had changed. She did not want to go home but did, limping like an injured animal back to her bed.

And it was no surprise later when Sissy refused to acknowledge her in school.

"Damn. Just…*damn*."

Van Daan stared hard at the girl, this strange creature that looked like any other child, until the words came out. He tracked the movement of her hands as she spoke, relying on the wall to hold him up. Initially, Daisy hadn't wanted to talk at all, but it was like digging water from the ground: the first few puddles led to a well. She was a running stream now, speaking hushed and haltingly, using her hands to say what her voice could not.

The Chief wandered in and out, looking only toward the finish and unconcerned with all the proceedings before, but van Daan had been rooted in place from the beginning, listening ravenously. Occasionally, he would jot a name or a date or a detail down, something that could be used late to close a file or start a new case.

So far, there had been plenty.

The medical report had completed their assessment of Mrs. Flanders's condition. All indications suggested she'd broken her hip from force and not a fall, and the amount of bruising across her hips, forearms and stomach indicated a beating. As thin as her skin was, it tore frequently during the assault, and she lost a substantial amount of blood. Of course, the nursing home would not acknowledge these injuries when van Daan called on the phone—the lady switched to Spanish at one point, and van Daan snarled at her. Then the line went dead.

Phone records indicated that three calls had been placed in the Flanders house that night: one to a cell phone that they knew was Daisy's mother; one was the 911 call that Daisy had placed, which could be retrieved on recording; and the third they eventually traced to a cell phone. Naturally, Daisy had been reluctant to identify who the call was to.

"Jesus Christ." Van Daan palmed his face, overwhelmed. Hard as it was, he tore himself away and stomped down to the Chief's office, pad in hand. He tried to hold himself like Martinez would as he listened to the girl quaver, erect and straight. He gave up after he rounded the hallway.

"Did Bobby Jenkins die from his injuries?" van Daan asked as he walked in. They were enough hours into the work to skip formalities. The Chief was at his desk poring over a file. The picture of an autopsy shot was in the top left corner.

"Looks like it," the Chief said. "Bled out. Collapsed lung, broken ribs. Died hard."

Van Daan swore. "And we're going to believe this little twerp who says she had *nothing* to do with this shit? You *heard* the part where she admitted she held the bat, right?"

The Chief cleared his throat and bridged his fingers. "Everything she's said has been on point so far, and she hasn't gone back on any of it. With her statement, we could close up some cold cases, and that's just the start of it." He looked evenly at van Daan. "And of course she's lying about her level of involvement. Fear and intimidation will do that. You know that. At the very least, she's an accessory."

"And the boys?" countered van Daan. "They accessories too?"

"They're a couple of fools tagging around with a crazy rag is what they are," the Chief replied gamely. "But, yes, them too."

Some digging had been done on the Jimenez brothers. And the little hellion, Avia—Avia Lynn Brutus. She and her cohorts had spent a few semesters together at Golden Hill, where they earned GEDs and got job training. It had been noted that, during this time, all three had listed the Flanders house as their residence, confirming the belief that Mrs. Flanders had fostered the brothers at some point.

Jesus and Tommy were foster care cases, separated, reassigned, repackaged, and regrouped at different intervals over the course of their adolescences. Avia had a father, Bernie Anderson who lived in small town forty miles away. Even though he'd held down a job and a house for most of her life, Avia's home address was her aunt's house—she grew up there, attended school from there, and apparently brought other strays there as well.

Burning a classmate with a cigarette got her expelled from Pleasantville High. Low aspirations and generational poverty kept her bouncing from place to place after that. Had Martinez been able to come up for air, he probably would've said that it was no coincidence Daisy fell in with those kids. By design of her own fractured upbringing, she shared the same DNA as Avia and the boys. For all her awkwardness, Daisy must have fit in like the last piece of a puzzle.

When van Daan came back, they were still going at it—the girl mumbling and illustrating with her hands and Martinez listening, completely unaffected by what he heard. Van Daan registered the relief he felt, being on his side of the glass. "Kids these days. Monsters, the lot of them." He chuckled humorlessly.

Some nights later, she awoke in a haze to the feeling of a hand stroking her brow.

Avia was murmuring, low and soothing, but Daisy couldn't understand any of it. Maybe it was the sheets constricting her or the hand smoothing her hair, but the air was cold and she was on fire. Sleep had not come easily for her; she doubted it ever would again. She must have made a noise at some point, because Avia shushed her and murmured again. Eventually Daisy turned and saw the outline of Avia lying on the bed beside her.

"I wanted to check on you." Avia scratched Daisy's scalp with her nails. She was lying on her side, facing Daisy, who lay on her back with her hands folded loosely across her front, open-casket style. Avia seemed to be rocking back and forth, looming over her and leaning back in equal turns. "Past couple days been hard on you, I get that. I want you to know I'm sorry. But it's all going to work out, don't you worry." She hummed tunelessly and swayed forward until she fell halfway across Daisy and lay on her stomach. An arm came out and slumped over Daisy, pulling her into Avia's side.

They had given her a wide berth after Bobby Jenkins. Food had been left on the counters of the kitchen, and a new hoodie lay draped across the arm of the living room couch. Daisy had not seen Avia come and go but knew it was her all the same. She hadn't gone outside, hadn't made any calls—who did she have to call, anyway? They had probably gone out hunting parts without her, and she wondered how much money she'd missed out on with a shame so fierce it burned.

Avia was rocking her slightly, or trying to, but she hummed and mumbled loud enough to keep Daisy from drifting off. Daisy guessed that Avia hadn't snuck in just to comfort her. She breathed in the smell of her cheap perfume and waited, as usual, for Avia's signal.

"What happened was bad, but it had to be done." Avia sounded certain.

Daisy nodded and marveled inside. How could one be so certain of something so terrible? And Bobby had never actually admitted to any wrongdoing. She could close her eyes at any time and still see Bobby Jenkin's skull cracked like a rotten cantaloupe, Avia's heavy breathing echoing in her ears.

But Daisy didn't have to close her eyes to remember the pungent odor of blood, and the image of Mrs. Flanders's nightgown soaked red, wetted down like a tissue in a puddle. She had gotten blood under her fingernails and scrubbed until she was confronted with her own blood. And it happened again the morning after Bobby's beating. How had she gotten it? Her mind had churned and savaged itself as she struggled to find an answer. She thought of nothing else, sleeping or waking, but no matter how her mind struggled to achieve resolution, she couldn't figure it out. But Avia was there, holding her fast and intoning her orders without hesitation.

If Avia said they had done the right thing, Daisy would have no choice but to accept it as fact.

"I know you never saw nothing like that, and know I never wanted you to see it. But I don't want you to be getting any funny ideas about me. Not at all." Avia smuggled a hand under Daisy's back and cradled her close until Daisy exhaled against her chest. "I want you to understand that about me. I'm not like that for no reason. Cruel, I mean."

She held Daisy and rocked her like an estranged mother forcing her love on a child. But Daisy had sunk so low that she actually leaned in and let the warmth consume her in a blaze. Eventually, Daisy found herself lulled into dim sleep.

The sleepiness is what almost made her miss it. Lips pressing against her hair, pressing down insistently until the small scab of heat was searing into her skull. The lips did not retreat slowly, but pressed down like a signature, like a proclamation. Daisy accepted the sensation. It was as easy as the ebb and flow of her chest and the even tempo of her heartbeat. Her head was so full she almost missed Avia's next words.

"But things are definitely going to be different from now on. Might be something to come from what we done. What *we* done, Daisy darling." The arms holding Daisy close locked her in place. "You, me, and the boys. This is a team and a family. You hear me?" Fingers dug into the minute space between them, searching for her chin. "Whatever happens, we handle it together. Always."

Perhaps Daisy was a fool. The truth was that she wasn't truly a loner; she was simply alone. Falling through the cracks had always been her signature move, even with—she'd suspected, feared, accepted—her own mother. Her mother, who called less and less nowadays; her mother, who was forever a silhouette in someone else's doorway.

Avia continued to rock Daisy, and Daisy fit into the fold of her arms as though it had been hollowed out for her. Avia continued to hum, and in her skin Daisy recognized a lullaby; the grooves in her hands and arms were the same as Daisy's, like their shared memories of barbed-wire fences and unforgiving gravel. A transformation had been completed. Avia had promised a team and offered a family; she had established a shelter and guaranteed a home. Avia needed only to point in the direction she thought was best and Daisy would do her damndest to stick to the path.

"Together," she said, and Avia nodded once with finality. And the deal was struck.

NOVEMBER

"DID YOU HEAR WHAT HAPPENED to the Selma girl?"

"Doesn't she have a twin?"

"Marissa. Yes."

"I heard she got married."

"No way in hell. She's, like, thirteen."

"No she wasn't. And anyway, she *had* to. Got knocked up and had to go out of state."

"What for?"

"What the hell you think?"

"Coulda gone two towns over, she woulda fit right in."

"Yeah, well she couldn't show her face around here. Not anymore. Not after what happened last summer."

"What happened last summer?"

Sissy Tompkins was always trying to sound like she knew more than she did. Upon returning from the summer and entering high school, she made a show of smoking cigarettes whenever she could, particularly when the junior boys from Sissy's block were present. Had Avia been watching, she would've mocked the way Sissy gagged on the smoke and told her she wouldn't impress anybody holding the cigarette at an angle that made the ashes land in her face. But Daisy was no Avia, so she simply nodded and rolled her eyes when Sissy gave her cues.

Avia had few hard values, but the ones she had she maintained religiously. Avia had insisted Daisy return to school and made a point of monitoring her attendance. Daisy's mother took her shopping for clothes three weeks into the school year, and Avia took her again the week after that, filling in the gaps her mother begged off. Often Avia would stand by while Daisy completed her homework in the evenings, checking each page before humming distractedly and waiting for Daisy to move on to the next assignment. Undoubtedly Avia's favorite subject to shadow Daisy in was English; any reading section she brought home had to be read aloud, most often on the dark neighborhood roads during scrapping nights with a flashlight, and Daisy tried her best to make the words come alive, if only to bask in the pleased, unwavering attention that Avia radiated as long as the pages lasted.

"I always loved a good story," Avia sighed one night, stretching in her car seat. It was remarkable to hear the wistfulness in her tone. One of Avia's favorite sayings was that one should never languish over the unattainable or the lost. "Probably the only good things about school for me. Always tried to find myself in the stories, you know? A used-up girl like me." She smiled and thumbed through Daisy's textbook. "Total waste of time." She laughed unrepentantly.

That Avia would be so dismissive of her own education and still be so insistent of Daisy's own was their only bone of contention. School was an institution that told you what to do and how to do it, where to go and who to be during the best parts of a person's life: Wouldn't it be better to skip all that? Daisy could leave school, find a side job, and learn a trade—seek her fortune, as Avia always said. School didn't teach you how to decode the lies and hypocrisy of the real world, and no class ever taught you how to reach inside yourself to find the strength to stand on your own two feet. Shouldn't Daisy be looking for a way to start her life, rather than just keep prolonging the inevitable?

Avia shook her head even before Daisy had finished. "You ain't been listening to a word I said." The school, Avia said, would give Daisy the tools she needed to plan the rest of her life; while she may have thought getting a diploma would be a waste of time—hell, even if she may have been right—the point still remained that not being in school was the *bigger* waste of time. "Yes, the world can be harsh, and yeah, it probably is a waste of time to be a body in a chair. There are still worse ways to spend your time.

"Look at those two." Avia jerked her head at Tommy and Jesus in the kitchen behind them. Jesus was rationing out potato chips into a bowl that lay cupped in Tommy's hands as though it were a newborn babe. "Complete losers, the both of them." Avia turned away and faced Daisy. "No, don't look at me like that. It's true and you know it. You got eyes in your head, and I know you see it." Behind them, Tommy spilled chips on the floor and hastened to pick them up when Jesus snarled. "Brothers, yeah, but Tommy's bled in the head, and it's Jesus' lot in life to look after him. Been that way since I known them and will probably always be that way. Ain't you noticed Tommy never talks?" Avia shrugged and her jagged hair, dull auburn and unnatural from the faded dye, skittered in its place on her brow. "He don't have the words to make a conversation, and Jesus is ashamed to have him try."

On scrapping nights, Tommy sometimes drove the car. He would navigate the car as though it were a beast fighting to free itself, slowing down to a dead crawl on the turns and the untextured dirt roads. During those times, Jesus sat next to his brother, and they shared as much of the driver's seat as they could, with Jesus going so far as to steady Tommy and seize the steering wheel from him when they veered too far off-road. In the months she had known them, Daisy could never recall the brothers speaking to her, but they never stopped talking—in their own nonverbal way—to each other. Theirs was a language hatched from emotion and familiarity, and Daisy had always been able to recognize and accept when she wasn't welcome.

"Jesus would be in school if time would let him," Avia continued. "What fool wants to baby their brother and have them run behind for a whole lifetime? It's pure misery." Avia turned away and made for the staircase. "You would do well," she didn't bother to lower her voice, "to remember you still got options, and for right now, you still got something to do and somewhere to be."

Daisy sighed and rolled her shoulders. Turning back to Sissy, who was just beginning to show the motions that her story was fast approaching its exciting conclusion, Daisy noticed a piece of spinach plastered to Sissy's front teeth and wondered that she couldn't feel it when she smacked her lips. Salads were the new trend she was embracing, her and all the other girls in their homeroom class. Before, it had been all about trying to get as much good food as they could for as long as it would last, but now—cheerleaders, parties, liquor runs, and boys who had cars and promises—getting fewer calories meant having fewer calories to burn off. "It's all about image, girl. See that one over there? You don't see her stuffing her face—ever. She's got it all figured out, though. Just watch." For her part, Daisy agreed, gave all the right affirmations and ate her pizza and cheeseburgers with relish. She got seconds every chance she got.

In English class, the first major project was a study over figurative language using a poem Daisy had read in the seventh grade. In advanced algebra, the first set of concepts introduced had been included in the summer package the high school had issued to all the freshmen enrolled in the honors program. Her world history teacher had opened with a long speech and a lengthy syllabus but tended to give up halfway through the period and would end the period at his corner desk, reading the newspaper and breathing heavily. Avia told her just to get what she could out of school and keep up with her reading, and her mother simply said she was too smart for her own good. It had been easy to hope that school and her classes would be different, that Daisy would find an identity in her studies and in the hallways of her new school. In the end, it was only the same song and dance as middle school. Daisy felt the disappointment keenly but was not altogether surprised. It was one loss among many.

The cafeteria always had seconds available, though. Daisy was grateful for that.

"So she's not coming home at all."

"Not at all?"

"No. No, she said she can't get off work."

"She works?"

"At the home. I told you, she cleans."

"Ah. Right. Those old geezers don't stop messing in their beds and dying just because it's Turkey Day, right?" Avia barked a laugh. "All right, then. So what are *you* going to do to celebrate?"

Daisy shrugged, the movement lessened from her position on the couch. She and Avia slouched shoulder to shoulder in the Flanders's living room, watching sitcom reruns. The boys were thunking around in the kitchen. The girls had cooked the night before, and Avia assured Daisy that for all his mulishness, Jesus could actually make passable pasta. The group took cooking in shifts because Avia insisted that the "gender inequality crisis" wouldn't affect her personally if she could help it—and cooking was always better than going out. "Cooking is what families do."

After a commercial with a dancing cartoon dog selling car insurance finished, Daisy felt nails scratching lightly down her scalp and knew she was being prompted to speak.

"Ruth talked to me last week," she said finally. "She said she couldn't be over in time for the actual holiday itself and the grocery budget didn't have a lot of room for any extra stuff, but that she would leave enough for dinner and leftovers on Thanksgiving night. She said she would stop by the next day, too, if I needed a ride anywhere."

Ruth had spoken to the counter as she made her offer, wiping down the weak stains with more care and attention than she normally did, and Daisy had been touched and entreated by the thin line of pride holding Ruth's shoulders straight as she spoke. Despite all the harsh talk and biting comments Avia would snarl at Ruth when she bothered to acknowledge her at all, Daisy had not outright refused the gift so carefully given. She understood how it felt to have little and still make the effort to give. Ruth had Daisy's respect for the gesture alone.

Avia scoffed but didn't actually argue, and Daisy was glad to avoid the confrontation. They went back to watching television long enough that Daisy thought the issue had been settled. Then she heard, "Your mom, Daisy darling. What's going on with her?"

Daisy thought long and hard before she answered. Most people would say that they wanted honesty and used this as an excuse to seek out ugliness in others. Avia was no exception: the uglier the truth, the more she reveled in it. She decided to give Avia what she wanted.

"My mother doesn't want to be a family," Daisy finally said, and it cut her throat to admit it.

Avia hummed and scratched deeper with her nails. Rather than protest, she simply said, "That why she never checks in?" And when Daisy nodded she hummed in affirmation. "Probably just as well, dear. You two spent so much time apart, you're practically strangers now. Say she came back tomorrow and moved back in, and you come in the door in the evening. Say she was, like, cooking dinner or some shit." Avia adopted her estimation of a mother's loving visage. "She'll say something like, 'Oh, child, where have you been? You had me worried sick.' Now," Avia cocked an eyebrow, "does that even seem real to you?" Daisy had to shake her head no and smiled back shakily when Avia beamed at her.

"People will tell you that families are made by blood, and that's a big fat crock. I mean, really, is that true for *every family* in the world? Family can be anything, anywhere, anytime. That's the gospel truth. You can sign it and book it." Avia smirked and pursed her lips, imitating a kiss. "You get what I'm saying?"

If Daisy could have had any family she wanted, then what? Her mother was her mother, the only one she'd thought she'd ever have. They had the same face and laugh; strangers had mistaken them for sisters. Avia was just a seat in the back of a car ducking in and out of darkness and the promise of a warm meal. She was blood under the skin. Before her mother had left, Daisy had never been so aware of the sheer possibility of all the bad things that could happen in a day. Avia had a shark's smile and rough hands. She claimed to have total control of her life and promised to teach Daisy the same. The single underlying truth, jagged and irrefutable, was that Daisy would never be completely safe in Avia's care.

But she would never be alone either.

Daisy looked over and Avia still had her lips pursed, wagging her eyebrows, making Daisy laugh despite herself and lean over. She accepted Avia's kiss and registered the warmth at her temple. "Thanksgiving?" she prompted, and they made plans for a feast.

"What did you eat?"

"Avia had the boys scrap an entire night so we could get a lot of fast food from like, seven places. We just went up and down the boulevard." She paused. "What did you do?"

He started. "What?"

"Thanksgiving. What did you eat? Did you eat?" She let out a small, skittered laugh. "Do you get to eat, or do you have to, I don't know, eat and drive? Because, I don't know, I would think that you might not get a break. The work never ending and all that."

"Oh." A soft smile creased his face with a bit of gentleness. "Some years I've had to work, but this year I was lucky enough to have that night off." It was his turn to pause. "I went to my sister's. She's a good cook, but not as good as my mother."

She returned a shy smile. "Where is your mother?"

"She passed. About ten years ago, actually."

"I'm sorry." She shrugged shoulders and leaned in. "My dad is dead. Or, he practically is: he's in prison. Life sentence."

He leaned in to mirror her. "I know."

DECEMBER

"COULD BE DRUG DEALERS, YOU** know. Peddle some shit here and there. Jesus has a cousin slinging it. Says he makes two grand a week. He would connect us if we wanted it. And hell," Avia took a long drag of her cigarette, "wouldn't be much different than this."

The arrival of winter, seated at last over Sweet Valley like a king on a throne, had brought no snow, only a stinging wind that rattled the cars and houses and stole the breath from people's mouths. Coated in a layer of ice and frost, the ground congealed like damp marble, and no birds screamed in the distance. The weathermen predicted rain showers from the televisions, but none ever came. Despite the infomercials about Pleasantville's new business boom in the downtown shopping plazas, the city seemed to be even more of a wasteland during the holidays. To fight the relentless cold, Avia declared the team would start their scrapping earlier in the evening, and they would cut their hours out of doors by half. It saved them money that would've been spent on gas, but it also shrank their pockets for everything else. No more nights spent at diners and drive-thrus, but for this Avia had another solution. "We'll lift it. Not more than we need—Christ, don't look at me like that. No, but we will need some stuff, and the haul is always dry this time of year. We can't afford to waste money we don't have on the essentials.

Which is why—"Avia handed the cigarette over— "we should look at another way to get some extra dough. Christmas coming and all that."

Daisy snorted. "Do you even celebrate Christmas, Avia?"

Avia snickered, and the girls traded a quick grin. "If I did, Daisy darling, it would be because you've had a bum year. Might not even know how much just yet." She turned back to her smoke and ignored Daisy's questioning glance.

Out of all the things that had happened, the incident with Patrick seemed to be the only one that Avia truly regretted. Stealing from the valley residents was for survival, and Bobby Jenkins had only gotten what he deserved. Patrick's indiscretion was an *embarrassment*. It was a needless crime, one committed by her actual family, and it was an affront to Avia's convoluted sense of justice. And, she said, it was only another mistake Patrick had made in a lifetime of screwing up that his mother, despite her efforts, had never been able to quash. Mrs. Flanders had employed prayer and medication to solve her son's defects. Avia said these were sucker's remedies and that Patrick wasn't a case that could be closed. So whenever they were all in the Flanders house at the same time, Avia made her intentions clear: Patrick was forced out of rooms, had his food snatched from his plate, was tripped as he crept past, and was almost thrown from the stairs one night.

Daisy could never be sure if the boys had any hand in it, or if Avia was just relieving her frustrations on her own. He would limp from his room or dash to the front door to get out of the house as Daisy and the others sat on the couch, and she knew better than to ask what inspired his fear. Avia sought justice for Daisy, demanding Patrick pay for his crime in the form of this torment. The hazing became so intolerable after a while that if Patrick happened to be in the house when Avia and the others came in, he would drop whatever he was holding on the spot and leave without a backward glance. Avia made it clear she did this for Daisy—not in words but in meaningful glances, as a way to atone for Patrick's foolishness on her behalf.

The decree was clear: since Patrick could not be counseled or removed, he would simply be made to suffer.

Daisy walked home from the Flanders house just as the sun was setting. Despite this new show of support, she never stayed in that house long enough for the evening to sink in and would only go over to visit when she knew Avia was there. Her own house was cold and empty, but for her, no matter the day or the occasion, the Flanders home was a tainted tomb. Regret lay in the stray pieces of clothing or the empty prescription bottles they sometimes found of Mrs. Flanders. Avia still slept there some nights, and Daisy couldn't fathom it. Mrs. Flanders hadn't been truly mourned, only messily avenged. But Avia simply said that her aunt had lived her life as best she could, and she would continue to do the same—at that house, just like any other.

Daisy let herself quietly through her front door. Tomorrow she could look forward to a movie in English based on a play they had finished, an open-book test in world history, and a volleyball game in the indoor gym, but all she could think about was getting some rest. As she drifted off, all the comforters in the house piled on her bed, her cell phone rang.

"Hello, sweet pea! What are you doing?" Her mother's voice was shrill and girlish.

"Sleeping." Daisy fairly grunted the word.

"Oh, sorry, dear. Did I wake you? My little girl, so *responsible* and getting to bed at a decent hour. You got school tomorrow, right?"

Wouldn't you like to know? she wanted to snarl, but instead she sighed, long-suffering and unimpressed. "Yes, mom. Wednesday night, remember?"

Her mother said she was sorry, of course she knew, funny how the time flew, wasn't it? But, she said, she was coming back tomorrow and had a big surprise for Daisy and she wanted Daisy to be as excited as she was. "Seriously, sweet pea. This is big."

Daisy yawned and told her mother that was great, it was all great, she'd see her tomorrow, couldn't wait, goodnight. She hung up, cutting her mother off mid-sentence and dreamed that night of a long tunnel full of fog, deep as a well, and brimming with the unknown.

"It was a new man. She had a new man. A new boyfriend." She rolled her eyes but her mouth trembled. "How long was I out there alone? Nine months? Ten? And the whole time she was just—out there—working a job and playing house. And that guy was a train wreck, man, c'mon."

He studied his bridged fingers. "How did she tell you this?"

"That was the surprise. She came and got me from the house, talking in my ear the whole way. We got to the restaurant, and she just goes in and sits down with this dude at the table. He'd been waiting for us." She barked a hoarse laugh. "You should have seen him. God, but his hands were dirty. Who goes into a restaurant and doesn't even wash their hands? My mother's dream man, that's who." She cradled her face in her hands. "Damn, but we really are trash. It's like trying to reach for the sky with the whole world pulling you down." She looked up. "There was no settlement, you know. That was all a scam cooked up by that man. Her boyfriend, I mean. He told her they should sue the home for Nana's death. And she bought it, the stupid bitch."

He tried—and failed—to be stern. "Cut that out. Whatever she is, she is your mother."

She breathed in quickly and scrubbed her face with her hands. "My mother. Yeah."

Avia liked to sleep in cars. She liked to sleep outdoors, out in the open and, she insisted, in the woods. She claimed to have slept in a bevy of outlandish places, no matter the weather or season: on a boat in the middle of a lake, in the bathroom of a Greyhound bus she'd been smuggled onto, and—most spectacularly—an empty boxcar on a train, which Avia promised was easier to break into than most people thought. Most of the time Jesus left the junker unlocked in the Flanders driveway, but on the nights the boys were otherwise engaged, Avia jimmied open a car nondescript enough to avoid attention or retaliation and slept until the sun came up. Daisy searched for an hour in the dying light before finding her in an old Suburban parked next to a church.

The Suburban was missing a passenger door handle, and Avia sprawled out in the backseat, snoring softly. Daisy hoisted herself into the passenger seat and closed the door gently. For a long time, she only stared out the window. She listened to the rhythm of Avia's breathing in the small space of the car and the rippling wind outside and let her thoughts churn.

Avia knew she was there and woke up quickly enough. She stretched and coughed. "Swear, I thought there was a rat in here when I first popped it open. Holes enough in the cushions. Had to lie on my side because there was a spring digging in my ass." She flung her blanket off and pulled herself into the driver's seat. "What is it now, Daisy darling? Looking like your dog died."

"What was your mother like, Avia?" Daisy was looking at a parking lot and still thinking about the plate of lukewarm macaroni the waitress had handed her. She was hearing a family with twins arguing in the booth behind her in the dim lighting of the restaurant, but here on the quiet street, no one else was around. Just the two girls in the car. "You've never mentioned her. Where is she now?"

"Where all the messed-up misfits go," Avia replied easily, and then when Daisy looked over, "*Jail*, silly. Been there since I was little. They got any sense at all, they'll never let her out, either." And when she could see that Daisy would not be so easily placated, Avia sighed.

"My mother is long gone, and it's good riddance too. Even before all that shit that went down, she skipped out on us all the time. One time there was a fire, and she had the nerve to blame me. Can you believe that? And after that—" Avia cleared her throat. "It would've been better if she'd always been gone. My little sister had a tough time coping with it; she wanted a whole family. Me, I was happy to let her go. She wasn't any good for us anyway." Avia's face closed neatly. "There was some other stuff too. But that's all over now."

Daisy nodded numbly. She should've cursed her mother out and watched it shred her mother's enthusiasm. Instead, she'd sat lifeless as a stone struck dumb by the fleshy arm slung around her mother's thin shoulders. Something in the way the man sucked and smacked his gums reminded Daisy of the cartoons she'd seen as a little girl of the fish that lived at the bottom of the ocean—a bottom feeder. The whole meal was a gaudy charade, and at any moment Daisy had hoped that her mother would erupt into laughter and they would leave together like the whole thing was a joke. The man—Randy, her mother supplied with the audacity of pride—asked her questions about school and told Daisy that her mother was a wildcat, an *absolute wildcat*. Daisy could've vomited on both the happy couple and their table. She could've grabbed her fork and speared Randy right through his sweaty forehead. She could not choke her food down. They asked her repeatedly to eat, and she stirred the food on the plate around.

Daisy looked at Avia. "I can't believe what a fool I've been." When Avia nodded sagely, Daisy added, "I've never been so angry or hated someone so much." They sat there quietly and felt the night shift around them.

Finally, Avia said, "You hate your mother because you think she betrayed you. Like, she just up and became someone else on you. Truth is, she hasn't changed at all. She always been this person, and you're just now seeing it." Avia lit a cigarette, puffed once, and passed it over.

They smoked silently, passing the pack back and forth, and in the quiet Daisy decided she would no longer stay in the empty house she had still thought of as home. She would no longer sleep in that cold bed or wait around in that dank desolation for old fantasies to come. She would sleep in cars, eat on the run, and shower in the spare times. School, when she could make it, would always be a short walk away. In clear, final words, Daisy told this to Avia with a voice she felt coming from beyond herself. Avia agreed at once and only said she'd been expecting it for a long time.

"She hates you, you know," said van Daan, aching to be cruel, and the woman's reaction did not disappoint: Her face caved in on itself, and she clutched it in her hands.

At some point, van Daan guessed it would be a good idea to let Ms. Sims in on the interview proceedings. Who better to tell her how Daisy had been getting by the past year than Daisy herself?

And the longer Daisy talked, the livelier her affect became. In any other situation, at any other time, van Daan might have guessed that the violence and depravity Daisy had experienced would cleave her in two as she let the words out. If anything, she seemed to draw strength from reliving it: her skin became less sallow, her voice less faint. Ms. Sims seemed to be mortified, and rightly so, van Daan thought.

As a sullen, pimpled youth van Daan had gardened alongside his father, and of all the activities they did together, he remembered hating the replanting— the digging and tending and cutting and moving and grooming—of the family garden, particularly the rosebushes his father loved. "Nature cannot always be surrendered to its own intentions," his father had said, and explained the ways roots could mangle themselves in the soil without proper guidance.

Looking through the one-way glass, van Daan saw that the youth talking animatedly with her hands was all thorns and no bud. He thought it more fitting than anything he'd learned so far, and so he goaded Ms. Sims to tears.

"Bet you wish you'd bothered to call more often now," he sneered, and did not care to hear what she said in response. He focused instead on the sentimentality splayed across Daisy's face and the way her hands cupped some unseen object. No matter how real or not it was, she would never let it drop.

JANUARY

AT THE START OF THE year, things began to change.

Jesus had a girl he was seeing in the down time, and it was a revolution. How could he net a girl, with Tommy tethered to him and the girls hanging close behind? But with the winter ice finally cracking and melting came a vacancy in the driver's seat of the junker, and Jesus began withdrawing his share of their scrap money. It took them an age and a day some nights, driving slowly down the roads with Tommy trembling at the helm. Without the other brother to complete the pair and guide him through the intricacies of everyday life, Tommy was cast adrift, a senseless child flailing and connecting with no one. He did not speak during meals and seemed to sink into heartbreak.

Avia made no effort to prize him from his grief, unforgiving as ever. She wanted Tommy's hopelessness to be an example for Daisy. "We have to stick together," she said grimly one night.

Daisy was adjusting the dashboard light to illuminate her homework but made a point of humming noncommittally.

"*A house divided against itself cannot stand.* Haven't we already established that? Spending money on that bitch—doesn't he give a damn about his brother, out here with us? And what about us, now? How fair is that to us, carrying on like this? Scrapping out in the wild—Tommy's going to cool the heat against us if we get caught, is that it? The freak'd piss his pants if you so much as looked at him funny. The hell do we do now?"

If Daisy found Avia's indignation unreasonable, she never said so. The fact was, having less money in the pile meant less money for food and gas, and the girls didn't know how to help Tommy, and he wouldn't have accepted it if they tried. The fact that Jesus' new squeeze—for whom he gelled his hair, donned new shoes, and bought or stole a crisp new leather jacket—came from a family of money only complicated things.

Her name was Emily, which was proper enough. She and Jesus met at a party, and Jesus persuaded her to let him walk her home. He helped Emily sneak back into her house, and they met again over the course of weeks under the guise of charity: Emily was filling hours at a community center as a tutor to add another credit to her college applications, and Jesus showed up and feigned interest in vocational programs to get close to her. Their song and dance was stilted and lacked societal finesse. Jesus would never be invited to dinner to meet the parents, and Emily would never be vetted by leering buddies who laughed and baited her. Nonetheless, theirs was a mutualistic relationship, the barest bones of a bond. It was a cheap kind of love with all the charm and ambience of a high school locker room.

Avia said the whole thing was pathetic. "He's a plaything, something she can pick up and drop whenever she wants. Can't he see how cheap that is?" Avia accused Jesus of losing focus and abandoning his family. She raged that he was destroying the routine they had worked so hard to establish, but Daisy knew enough to know that the real condemnation lay in Jesus allowing himself to hope.

Avia said the relationship would go up in flames. Daisy agreed and didn't feel sorry for Jesus in the least. Life was hard everywhere. Not even Avia had to tell her that.

"What are the odds we'll be able to find them?"

Van Daan groaned, and the Chief's scowl deepened. He didn't want to say their chances were slim—no trail of addresses or employers to uncover, no family or associates to interview. The three of them had been self-contained— and remarkably so, living as they did and getting by so long with so little interference. Van Daan admired his quarry even as they made his job difficult.

Avia's mother was, in fact, serving a life sentence in prison for arson and attempted murder. Daisy fit so well into the mold that made Avia that they were practically destined to be together. Had Avia looked at Daisy and seen the likenesses? If that was the case, why abandon her? Because it was obvious that was what happened. There was a range of motivations to consider, but without Avia there in the flesh, it was near impossible to tell. Van Daan recalled the nature shows he binge-watched at home and thought again of the girl's thin, almost fragile frame. The weak were always the first to die. Neither the young nor the old were ever completely safe.

"I honestly don't know how much luck we'll have," van Daan said "I mean, by all accounts they just up and vanished, boss. If anyone could tell us, it'd be the girl, but…" Van Daan paused to find the words. "But I don't think she'll tell us."

"Loyalty?" the Chief asked, and van Daan nodded. The Chief swore slowly, and van Daan repeated the sentiment.

"Go on in there in a minute and help close it in," van Daan heard after a minute. "Been quite awhile now. He'll need the support."

Looking back in through the glass, van Daan felt like a cat lusting after an elusive bird. They were so close. At first van Daan couldn't see that any time had passed for the pair in there, one unloading a year's worth of memories and terrors in a burst like spirits from the possessed, the other sifting through all the objects, weighing and waiting patiently. He felt like all he'd done all night was watch the girl, listening to her words and trying to see if they would reveal something else.

For the most part, Martinez had slouched in his seat, letting the words wash over him, only speaking to prod Daisy to continue. Now he was leaning in again, placing his palms down evenly on the counter and preparing his face—preparing his words to have a special gravity. The girl was not unaffected by it. At first she leaned away, until some magic forced her hand. Then she was leaning in too, bracing her hands against the edge of the table as if Martinez were physically pulling her. As soon as he heard the signal, van Daan was leaning in as well. He recognized the words and knew it was time. Martinez was closing up.

"—and then after that, it was like—well what do you really say to that, you know? So in the end, I just had to tell her that—"

"Let me stop you right there." He placed his palms on the table. "I've been listening to you, to your story, and at this point there's something I need to tell you."

She eyed him warily. "Spit it out."

"If I'm understanding the timeline correctly, Emily Burns died in mid-January. And by all accounts, you know something that can help us find her killer. You know it, and I know it." He met her stare evenly. "You buried items of hers in the lot close to where the body was found, and we found your DNA among them. Even without all that, you've already admitted—whether you know it or not—to knowing and having spent some time with Ms. Burns prior to her death." He gave a gentle smile. "Surely you talked to her at least once. Maybe she came and met up with Jesus once in between hanging with Avia and ditching you guys. What was she—friendly? Rude? Stuck-up, just a little? Probably a little prudish?"

"Like, in her clothes? She was definitely a little fancy, maybe. She wore everything name brand." Her eyes misted over, her lips trembled. "But she seemed nice. Pretty and nice."

"Do you know what she was wearing the night she died?"

"Yes… No."

"Okay." He'd play along. "Well, when we found her, she was dressed like she was going on a night on the town. Dressy clothes, you know. Black pants, blouse. Nice underwear." He noted her blush. "The kind of clothes girls wear when they really want to impress someone."

Her voice was faint. "Oh. Okay."

"That's not all we found, though." He paused. "Daisy, what does your room look like?"

"My room?"

"At your house. You must have decorated." He cleared his throat and renewed his smile. "Your mom didn't start going through jobless cycles until the last couple of years, right? And you've lived in the same house your whole life. Just tell me, I'm curious."

"What for? It's a room. No big deal."

"Well, sure, but"—he leaned in— "Emily was wrapped in a bed sheet. A girl's bed sheet too. Kind of a childish design, and—honestly? Kind of a print and make that wouldn't be Emily's style at all. Too cheap." Still leaning in, he watched her lean back. "What do you think about that?"

She roughly scraped back her chair. Lip clenched in teeth, she whispered. "Just say what you're going to say."

"I'd rather hear it from you." He leaned in further, flattened his hands, and allowed his smile to morph into a devil's grin. "C'mon. You've already said so much, Daisy, it's nothing just to tell it all. And when you do, it'll all be over."

She let out a sigh like she was dying. "Avia had a gun. She never told me where she got it. She said it was for protection. She'd always been a little jumpy, but it just got worse all the time. And then one day Jesus was supposed to pick us up to go get dinner, and he didn't show. Avia said he was with his girl and the distraction had gone on long enough. She was so angry. I told her just to forget it. I did—I told her just to drop it. I said, why don't we just go another night?"

But Avia wasn't giving her the time to breathe and Daisy couldn't wrench her arm free. "It'll work out, Avia, honest. A day or two won't make much difference. We can even go Friday, if you want. I'll skip school."

"Keep up with the press, Daisy darling, and open your goddamn *eyes*." Avia stopped abruptly and whirled around. The arm she was gripping was shaken in frenzy, and Daisy moved with it helplessly. "Do you see us walking? Do you? Strung out here like two bums in a field? It's going to be dark soon. We should not have to be doing this." Avia kicked at the ground viciously and grit her teeth. "This is the third time. This is the third *fucking* time he's done this, and it's the *last* time." She set off again, dragging Daisy behind her.

Daisy dug her heels in and tripped when Avia wasn't slowed "C'mon, Avia, please calm down. We'll go out tomorrow and scrap, just us two, if you want. Girls' night out. And besides," she said, drawing herself up, "he's entitled to his own life. You're being unfair." She took another step, and suddenly Avia's free hand was squeezing her face so hard it nearly broke the skin.

Avia leaned in, and Daisy was caught up in the torrent in those eyes, gray as the winter sky and just as lifeless. "You don't talk to me about what's fair and what's not." Her eyes bored in, and Daisy cowered. She stared back until her eyes watered. "I'm not out here because life is fair. I'm out here because someone is letting me down, and I won't stand for it." She released Daisy, turned and stalked off. Daisy followed.

They circled the three blocks between Daisy's house and the Flanders place. Avia insisted on circling so that no spot was left unsearched, so the girls would catch Jesus immediately. There was no sign of the junker, and by the time they finally decided to turn back, the valley had been fully submerged in nighttime cold. Avia lounged on the couch and raided the refrigerator to calm down, and Daisy, worn out from searching and wrung dry by Avia's vitriol, could only stumble up the stairs to her bed. They had less than an hour alone in the house before Jesus' junker chugged onto the driveway, setting Avia raging anew.

But rather than storming outside and confronting Jesus directly, Avia let herself out through the back door and darted out of sight. Daisy knew she was headed for the shed in the backyard and didn't follow. Should she go out by herself and brace for confrontation? No, she waited from her place at the top of the staircase for Avia to return so they could fight it out together.

But Avia didn't return. Daisy stayed resolute, but anxiety gnawed at her. She crossed the hall and looked out the window. She saw the shed, the door cracked slightly ajar. The open shed door and the silence downstairs unnerved her. Slowly, seeing no one, Daisy came back downstairs and went into the kitchen. The back door hung open. Daisy shuddered and crept to the backyard. She stood and listened for sounds that were not there, and after a few tense minutes, noises from upstairs echoed back to her and signaled the beginning frenzy. She rushed back inside and bounded up the stairs.

They were in the guest bedroom. Daisy had slept there, once. There was a thud and shouts that intensified as she topped the staircase. The door was firmly shut. Even then, she could've turned and ran. But instead, she opened the door and let herself in.

Jesus was holding Avia down at the arms while she lunged and snarled and tried to dislodge him. The girl had her back to the door and was putting her clothes on hastily, tripping and missing buttons and muttering under her breath. The bed was a tangled mess. Jesus' pants hung low on his hips, almost falling to his knees as he and Avia struggled.

Avia never seemed to stop for air; it was a wonder she could scream so much. "How could you do this" and "how long has this been going on" and "why couldn't you be honest with me." And then, drawn darkly from the bottom of her: "What are we supposed to do now?" Jesus never answered. He held Avia in place and didn't even seem to see her.

When she was presentable, the girl, Emily, turned around. It was a pretty blush that pooled in her cheeks, the seed of a woman-to-be already dancing in her eyes. She smiled politely, and Avia froze.

"I think I should be going now." There was a fancy purse on the bed. She grabbed it and tucked it under her arm. She crossed the room and brushed against Jesus and Avia simultaneously, smiling brightly and laughing when Jesus leaned against her. It seemed her intention not to acknowledge Avia directly, and Avia waited, coiled to spring until the girl reached the doorway, where Daisy stayed frozen. She smelled clean, free of any perfume, and her hair fell artfully about her shoulders. "Oh, hello there, you must be Daisy." She laughed again, softer and warmer this time. "Jesus was actually telling me about you. Funny thing, but he told me you were ugly as sin." Daisy looked at her and slowly realized: The glaze in her eyes and the glow of her face was distorted, like looking at one's reflection with cracked glass. Was she drunk? Probably not, but she was buzzed. Or high. Looking over at him, Daisy could see it in Jesus' face too.

"Leave her out of this." Avia spoke softly and without any real fight in her voice.

Emily didn't look back at her but tilted her head slightly and blinked slowly. "We want nothing to do with you. You have no business here, and neither does she."

The girl turned to Avia with a face that made her cringe. Daisy couldn't see the expression; her mind supplied a blank face. "He may have been wrong about her, but not about you." And she slid past Daisy, smooth as water. Hardly a sound as she headed down the stairs.

The three of them remained in place, watching her leave. Daisy waited helplessly for someone to say or do something to break the spell. Avia broke first with a sureness that belied all her unseen terror. She shucked off Jesus' restraining hold and stood apart from him, looking at him with wooden eyes. Then, before anyone could move or react, Avia turned on her heels and bolted out of the room.

It was like swimming upstream in a down current. By the time Daisy could react, Avia was nowhere to be seen. The front door opened and slammed shut once. Daisy moved sluggishly down the staircase, feeling blindly for the handrail. When she finally got to the front door, she could not fathom what she would find on the other side, but she did not give herself time for doubt; as she took hold of the handle and slowly opened the door, she took a deep breath. It came out in a gust as she beheld the scene in the yard.

Avia had Emily pinned against the side of the junker and was trying to slap her face. She had a hand wrapped around Emily's throat and was swinging her arm back and forth, but Emily dodged and bucked in Avia's clutch, laughing and wheezing but didn't try to free herself. The more Avia swung, the more Emily wriggled and laughed, so that one beast breathed life into the other. Avia's anger crested when she released Emily and reached into her back pocket. Emily, still giggling, sagged against the car and brushed her hair out of her face.

"Are you angry because he's with me?" she crooned to Avia, who held something close to her side Daisy couldn't see. "Are you *totally devastated*? I could have guessed this would happen. You poor thing." Avia didn't answer, only took a single calculated step back. How odd it was to suddenly see her so calm and steadfast. She had snarled and snapped at any opportunity all week, all month, all *year*; anger was a language Avia spoke fluently. How strange it was to see her so detached now, when perhaps she'd never needed her anger more.

Emily's laughter died in her throat as Avia leveled the gun evenly between her eyes. Nothing happened immediately. Avia was adjusting the weapon in her hand, and Emily was struggling to understand exactly what she was looking at.

Shouldn't Jesus be coming down? Daisy locked down the urge to scream and run back inside. Hysteria waited in her blood, ready to bloom. She stood in her spot in the open doorway and prayed that no one would happen to chance a glance outside their windows and screen doors to see what was happening that night.

A few more moments and Emily began trembling uncontrollably. She collapsed against the car, unable to stay upright. That was when Avia relaxed enough to lower the gun to her side. The physical admission of Emily's terror was sufficient to assuage her. With the threat temporarily suspended, the debutante surrendered to frantic sobs.

Avia watched her cry and made no effort to comfort her—or finish her off. They stood there for what felt like eternity. Daisy's blood cooled, and her insides writhed. Why wouldn't she pull the trigger? Daisy guessed that Avia might've wanted to maximize the pleasure of that moment, finally beating this girl who had so much and demanded so much more. But when Daisy looked, she could find no true presence in Avia's eyes. She stood with her feet planted, shoulders level, but Avia had never before held a gun, and she swam in her own indecision.

For her part, Daisy felt helpless and miserable. She would not raise a hand to stop Avia, but the night was wearing thin. If it had to happen, Daisy prayed it would be quick. *Please, please let it be quick. Let it be over soon.*

With only half of Avia's face visible, Daisy couldn't be certain of anything. But Avia had never been one to doubt herself before. And now her opportunity had come and gone. If Avia hadn't already decided to go through with it, she wasn't going to. The relief was immediate. Daisy took a breath that rattled her chest and took a step down from the porch.

Avia heard her coming and turned to her, a question on her face. Before Daisy could say anything, Emily was suddenly screeching and lunging—shoving Avia with all her might, scratching at her face and knocking her down—Avia with her face hidden, cursing and flailing, digging blindly in the grass for the gun, unable to withstand Emily's fury.

As soon as Daisy's fingers touched the cold metal, she lost her mind. That was a defense they used in court, right? She had never believed it, or even paid a thought to it before, but there was no other way to explain the way she knew to cock the lever and find the trigger. There was no other way to explain her coming closer, smooth, even steps that did not falter, and standing over the two girls.

They did not see her. Emily was making spitting sounds, and Avia was cursing low and fierce, her face bloody and swelling—Emily trying her hardest to scratch her eyes out, Avia with red knuckles trying to throw her off. And there was no time, no possible time to think, no way to pull them apart or scream at them to stop. How could she scream louder than their own screams, anyway?

And how did the neighbors never hear it? And the blood, so much blood that it was a wonder it wasn't dripping off Emily's blouse or flooding the lawn. And now Emily's yips were morphing into a maniacal, howling kind of laugh that shredded Daisy's eardrums in her skull, Avia cursing low and steady, steady like a metronome, scratching her fingernails down to the nub and still bucking, flailing like a chicken with its head cut off.

Jesus would not be coming down, and it was all his fault anyway, casting them out into the ungodly night like trash so he could sweep this princess off her feet, staying up there in that bedroom, probably looking down on them and laughing his head off.

There were marks forming up and down Avia's arms and neck, and how was Emily not hoarse from that inhuman *laughing*? It simply had to stop, and no one else was around, and it had to be Daisy, it had to, it had to, *it had to*. The cops would be there any moment, the girls would not be quiet, and if the situation wasn't handled it would be Daisy's responsibility, it would, it would, *it would*—

The gunshot was the single loudest thing she'd ever heard. It erased any other sounds in the entire valley and seemed to obliterate everything it touched. Beneath the dead girl, Avia was barely breathing, her eyes filming as she looked at Daisy. She had stopped thrashing immediately, but still held the body by the arms in a loose hug, still staring into its lifeless face.

Daisy, bowed and on her knees before her, wanted to be reassuring. She wanted Avia to comfort her, calm her, so she said the only thing she could think of.

"It had to be done. Please, it had to be done. I know what you're thinking—"

"I don't think you do."

"—but it had to be done. That girl, Emily, she was crazy, she would have killed her. They would have killed each other. Please, I know what it means, but I'm just telling you what it is." She reached for his hands.

He retreated from her grasp. "What happened to the gun?"

She was silent, then: "I don't know. I never saw it again."

"What did Avia tell you to do with the body?"

"She didn't. Jesus did."

Now he paused. "What?"

"Jesus came down, saw Emily. He'd been watching from the window upstairs. The sheets from the guest bed—he brought them down and told me to wrap her up. Then we put her in the trunk, and Jesus said he would do the rest. He—" she swallowed hard—"She had plastic nails. Kind of like Avia's. Jesus cut them off, washed her face. There was a lot of blood. At the time I thought he was just paying respect."

"Did he say anything else to you?"

"He said he was sorry. For everything. He said I didn't deserve any of it, and I shouldn't ever blame myself."

"What did Avia say?"

"Nothing, that's just it. She just looked at me."

Avia's face looked as mangled as Daisy's insides. The morning sun, leisurely topping the trees and hills, touched over the earth in a light caress. No way would this night not leave scars. Daisy did not dwell on it, reminding herself that Avia always said scars were evidence of an interesting life.

Hours had passed since the horror, and Avia still wouldn't speak. Jesus was already gone. Daisy could only assume he'd gotten the shovel from the Flanders's shed. He never told her he blamed her for what happened and showed no malice toward her in those few surreal moments. He'd even touched her face before he left—grazed her cheek with the tips of his fingers but wouldn't look at her. Perhaps it meant nothing. Avia was still in shock, and Daisy's own mind was far afield.

Avia had been coaxed off the ground and back into the house easily but resisted all of Daisy's attempts to get her upstairs and into a bath. So Daisy brought the bath to her: She washed Avia's cuts and combed her hair, scrubbed the ugliness from under Avia's nails and held her hands, trying to draw her out of her stupor. It did not frighten her that Avia would not speak, not at first. Avia was still there, shoved away inside herself, but they had weathered such storms before, Daisy whispered in the dull, rough red hair. They would persevere and carry on—just like before.

Hours passed. Avia curled in on herself and slept. Daisy sat at the top of the staircase and kept watch. Jesus did not return, and the day that followed was altogether uneventful. There were no visitors. In the past few weeks, Patrick had begun to gradually disappear. She'd never given any indication of this, but Daisy suspected Avia had rooted him out permanently to make Daisy feel more comfortable. Even Ruth was gone, no longer making her charity visits anymore, and Daisy didn't answer her mother's calls. They were very much alone.

In the middle of the night, Avia awoke with a whimper. Daisy took the opportunity to hustle her up the stairs and into bed. She put Avia up in Mrs. Flanders's bed and tucked her in, and when Avia was finally settled, Daisy felt her weariness and lay down opposite her charge. She reached out and felt for Avia's hand, squeezed once to remind Avia of her presence and slipped easily into oblivion.

"She really is a good girl. A little lost, maybe. But a good girl. The other was a waste. She broke the family's heart." The words seemed to sit strangely in Ruth Ortega's mouth, as though she'd never gotten a chance to say them out loud. Perhaps that was the case, but van Daan suspected that no one had ever really listened to her at all. Mrs. Ortega sat rigid in the plastic chair; she'd never been in a police station before, she said, and seemed embarrassed to be there in her work clothes.

After Mrs. Flanders's accident and subsequent relocation, Mrs. Ortega got a job cleaning an office on the weekends. The Chief called her in for an interview because he wanted to see if Mrs. Ortega could be a viable character witness and could corroborate anything they'd heard so far. From what van Daan could gather, Mrs. Ortega would be of little use to them. She hadn't been in the Flanders house enough to notice what had actually been happening to Daisy and seemed only more sympathetic to her case the more she learned. Van Daan wrapped up their discussion quickly. He thanked Mrs. Ortega, guided her back to the lobby, and promised to call if they needed anything else.

Before she left, she grabbed van Daan's forearm and dug her fingers in with a sudden ferocity. "They *ruined* her," she intoned gravely. "Those other kids, that ugly girl. They destroyed her life. And now they are gone, yes?"

Van Daan agreed quietly because nothing else was appropriate, and Mrs. Ortega released him.

"Do what you can for her," she ordered, and left quickly, hurrying out to her husband, impatiently waiting in their pickup.

When van Daan returned, the Chief told him to pull Martinez out. "We've heard enough to move forward. Get him, and let's get on with it."

Reentering the interrogation room, Daisy struggled to recognize van Daan. She had lost him in those hours that had taken her somewhere else, to some faraway place inside her memory. Seeing him again brought her back violently; she jolted in her seat, brought her hands to her mouth with wide eyes. The words could not be taken back. The girl knew it, and the men saw it. Van Daan cleared his throat and gestured at Martinez without his usual brazenness.

"It's, uh, time. Chief called it." Van Daan stood by the table and waited for Martinez. Martinez moved slowly. If van Daan hadn't known him as well as he did, he would've thought that Martinez was hesitating, but he got up easily enough and exited without a single glance back. Van Daan was left to watch the girl.

"How do you do." He instantly felt strangely stiff and formal. She registered the strangeness of the comment, too, and looked at him like he'd grown a second head. He was being buried alive by his own awkwardness. He waited impatiently for his partner to return.

Martinez came back quickly enough. He let himself in quietly with eyes only for the child. He crossed to her side and held out a hand.

"Time to go, Daisy."

She looked first at the hand and then at his face. Van Daan found he was suddenly grateful. There was no fight left in her, and if there were no burdens left to bypass as soon as they cleared the hallway, Martinez could lead her away, and the process would begin, smooth and peaceful. *Please, let it all go peacefully.*

Ms. Sims was waiting for them as they led Daisy out. She reached for Daisy and might have said her name. Van Daan couldn't be sure because he was watching Daisy cringe and shy away from her mother's entreating hands, shuffling into Martinez like a frightened animal. Or maybe she was helpless against Martinez's arm, which swept around her and pulled her away. There was a car outside and another room, a series of rooms and hallways and chambers and doors that would soon lock her future away.

Chief watched from the doorway of his office with a hard sort of satisfaction. Van Daan looked at Daisy's curved back and searched for some feeling of his own in the dirt on her jeans and the oily sheen of her hair. Satisfaction was too crass, even for him. Sympathy was too cheap. He did not look at Martinez because he knew that that moment, more than any other, was the time to react without reacting at all.

After they left, the Chief presented van Daan with a stack of forms. "Might as well get it over with now." Van Daan wanted to protest, thought about it quite seriously. He was overcome with sentiment. He wanted to say that they needed to consider what would happen next, maybe try to offer the girl some assistance for what was to come. Just take a moment, even, pause for reflection. He wanted to *talk* about it with someone, hash it all out and come to an understanding with the Chief, since he doubted Martinez would be open and willing to reflect; he was the type to say things once and never again. But van Daan blinked once and knew that the moment was over, had already been over; and without another thought he wandered over to his desk.

It took him an hour and a half to fill out all the paperwork, but that was hardly any time at all.

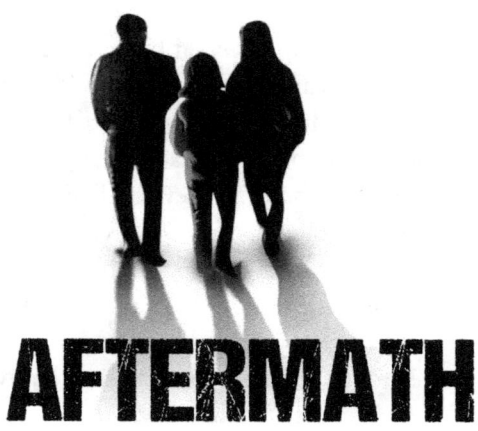

AFTERMATH

DAISY AWOKE AT THE CRACK of dawn on her edge of the bed and listened to the sounds of the body next to her. Avia hogged the covers and snored a little. Sometimes she would kick and roll from side to side in her sleep, but not this day. There were no other noises from downstairs and they were still alone.

Daisy thought and thought. They needed a plan for what they were going to do next. Obviously, getting rid of Emily and the evidence was the first step, but Jesus had seen to that, and now it was important that they consider what to do with themselves. Jesus and Tommy had not called or come back, but they would. Avia had not yet broken her silence. Daisy watched the light sifting in and felt solid and heavy as stone. Despite everything that had happened, there was no panic or fear; how could those things hold any power when Daisy had only fulfilled her responsibilities? *It had to be done.* And when Avia came back to herself they would get up and continue. Last night had been an obstacle, but they'd overcome it like all the others. Their path lay unchanged before them.

Probably their best option was just to pack up and jet. There were a smattering of small towns surrounding Sweet Valley, and they could have their pick of them. They could get money anywhere—junkyards dotted the gray-grassed hills no matter which direction they went—and they would need time to get a new setup. Sleeping in cars, crashing abandoned lots—this was their rhythm, and Daisy was ready. Let her mother have her bastard prince and discount romance; let her friends in that dropout factory entertain delusions while they strived for a cardboard diploma and dreams that would not come true. Daisy was ready to leave it all for a thousand more nights under a sky that was never the same twice. She would hit the ground running and never look back. But Avia needed to awaken first, and they needed to talk.

Eventually, Daisy turned and saw Avia awake and looking at her. She didn't hesitate: She launched into her proposals with an urgency that only increased the longer she talked. Avia listened so impassively that the words seemed to make no impact. Still, that didn't deter Daisy; her confidence was concrete.

She excused herself to go downstairs and hunt for some food. When she came back, Avia was dressed and looking around the room blankly. "Jesus will be back tonight." She didn't sound happy or angry; she didn't sound like anything. "I'll need to talk to him. He's got Tommy with him, so you keep him here and wait for us. We'll come back with dinner."

Daisy stared, and Avia didn't see it. Avia had never purposefully separated the group before. "Oh. Okay. Do…do you want me to do anything?" And then Avia turned around, and Daisy took a step back. Avia's face was closed, and her voice was soft.

"No, Daisy darling. We're good."

The junker rolled up in the drive not long after that. Avia got in and quickly left with Jesus. Tommy, deposited on the stoop, walked in and secluded himself in the kitchen, where his sniffles reverberated throughout the empty house. Daisy had to fight not to scream at him to be quiet. She waited, on edge, at the foot of the staircase for the junker to return. When it did that night, Daisy could see that a weight had been lifted off Avia as she approached the front door, and that lifted a weight off of her too.

They ate Thai takeout on the couch together, the four of them. Avia was light and lively again. They watched old game shows and sitcoms and tried to guess the punchlines before they landed. Avia threw her head back to laugh uninhibited. Daisy soaked in the familiarity of their routine like the warmth of a bath. It was a sensation that lingered as they retired for the night, the boys slinking off to some haven, and Avia and Daisy to Mrs. Flanders's old bed.

Avia said that it was to be their last night in the house. The bank was sure to come and seize the property. When they did, they would change the locks, and Avia was only surprised they hadn't done so already. Avia had given Daisy's ideas some careful thought and decided she was right. "But we can't go right away. You still have school, and it's not a lot of time left. Finish the month; you'll be glad you did in the long run."

Daisy argued but lost. She eventually agreed that she would go back to staying in her house until further notice and would even try to be a little nicer to her mother when she saw her. Surely, Avia said, her mother would come back. Sooner or later, she would return for her daughter, whom she loved so much. Tomorrow, Avia insisted. Daisy would go back tomorrow.

Avia and the boys would pick a spot and be gone by the end of the week. They would come for Daisy when the time was right. Avia promised Daisy all this with a hand scratching at Daisy's hair, lips pressing against her scalp again—the first time in so long, making Daisy's faith all the stronger—making everything right with the world, putting her at ease. When she woke up the next day to find Avia was already gone, Daisy wasn't worried. She went home, let herself in, and practiced busying herself to shorten the long wait.

The Chief was strangely impatient when Martinez came into his office from the interrogation room. "You about done? Need to get this packed and moved." He was talking about the girl.

Martinez heard the words and processed them, but he was unable to move his feet, and seemed, to anyone watching, noncompliant, rooted in place as though if he were still enough, he could disappear entirely.

The Chief was focused on his computer screen and did not see Martinez's hesitation. With his gaze away he grumbled, "Did *not* put much stock in your theory, but it looks like you were right. Found the Jenkins file too. Wrapping up multiples under one perp? That's a golden ticket." He looked at Martinez. "You did good. Van Daan'll mock up a statement. Have her sign it. I already called Williams over at the junction. We need to have her there in thirty."

Martinez was blank-faced. "Juvenile detention?"

"Best we can do for her." The Chief considered Martinez before adding, "The mother won't contest. She doesn't know everything. She can find out like everyone else. But the press will have to keep the circuit closed. It's a minor we're talking about here. They can be kept at bay."

Martinez nodded. In his mind, he was already making the drive down to the youth center. Tucked away in the eastern part of town, the outer grounds had been remodeled in the past year—all the better to avoid being an eyesore, since the facility's closest neighbor was an upscale shopping center. Martinez had been to the center before, of course. The head officer had a beard as dense as a forest and had a voice like crunching bark.

"You ready, Leonard?"

The Chief had been talking and Martinez hadn't heard. Did they need to get dinner before they left? The cafeteria was closed by now, and the vending machines were all either busted or empty, but there had to be a drive-in open somewhere. Couldn't send her to the center with an empty stomach; wouldn't be proper. Especially considering it might be the last for a long while. They could even get van Daan to get some takeout from a diner—and there Martinez had to stop and shake himself free of his reverie. Definitely not that.

No matter who could be watching, he did not take his time walking back to the interrogation room. Someone spoke to him in the corridor, and he stopped to answer their question, and he hadn't checked his emails or his desk in so long. He went to the restroom and then couldn't get up from his seat. He washed his hands twice. All these things took time, but Martinez took no second for granted, and through it all he thought of nothing. He couldn't. Every time he closed his eyes or stayed still too long he saw that bag of trash and trembling hands. He saw a jagged eyebrow scar and a gutted-fish stare.

Before he got down the hallway he solved it. He weighed the scales and remembered himself, remembered the purpose of it all. Martinez reminded himself only once, and then he was better. He was.

The end of the week came, and Avia did not come. Two weeks, and Avia did not come. The end of January came and there was no junker, no red hair freshly painted from a bottle, no jagged nails or chipped teeth. Instead, Daisy's mother came back and brought the boyfriend with her. The man immediately dented the left side of the couch and filled the house with the stench of beer, his only contribution to the home. Daisy waited with bated breath for them to leave and toppled into rages when they asked too many questions. Eventually, they began to drift from the house again with no explanations or false promises. Her mother continued to leave food and money, and Daisy pocketed the money at every opportunity. She ate the scraps until they ran out, hoarded leftovers from school and lifted everything else. She did not allow herself to fall into grief. Avia and the boys were obviously struggling to come up with the money for gas. Daisy would pay them back with all she had just as soon as they were reunited, as a token of her gratitude.

Daisy saw the first billboard for Emily Burns in February. She was in a car with her mother, going to the movies for some bonding time, just the two of them. It was a Saturday evening. They passed it on the overpass, and Daisy dropped her soda in her lap. Her mother had a spare jacket in the backseat and tied it around Daisy's waist so no one would see the mess on her pants. They watched a romantic comedy that had been her mother's pick, and Daisy could never remember afterward exactly what the movie was about.

Jesus had not gotten every little thing when he cleaned up and disposed of Emily. Little pieces of her had been left in the yard—a compact, which fell out of her back pocket; earrings—a cheap throwaway pair that Avia had somehow ripped out of Emily's ears. Daisy found them in the yard the day after Emily's death and hid them away. She never mentioned it to anyone because she never believed she needed to.

March came, and it was Daisy's birthday. Her mother baked a cake and asked Daisy if she wanted to invite any friends over to the house to celebrate. Daisy said no one would come to a house like theirs and sealed herself off in her room. The items she'd harbored, along with all the money she'd saved, were in an old tin of Mrs. Flanders's in the bottom of her closet. She'd needed to find a new place to stash her goods after she'd gotten out of the shower to find her mother's boyfriend waiting for her on her bed. On the night of her birthday, she let herself into the Flanders house for the first time in months and stowed the tin away. It was all the same anyway, she mused. As if that bum hadn't been enough, she suspected her mother had begun a new habit of going through her things, looking for drugs or something else exciting.

Crouched on her knees in the oppressive dark, Daisy breathed in hot musty air and prepared her collection. The compact, the earrings, a scrunchie she'd borrowed from Avia, and the disposable camera, a gift from Jesus to Tommy—the only kind gesture Daisy had ever seen pass between them. She hid the items away with a kind of reverence. They were necessary and holy for no other cause, save to serve as talismans Daisy used to preserve her fading hope.

Jesus hadn't really given Tommy the camera. Not on his own, anyway.

It was a joint gift, really, from both Jesus and Avia. Avia got it from the corner store around Christmas time. She'd lifted gifts for all of them: Jesus got an MP3 player, Tommy got the camera and a puzzle, and Daisy got the sleeping bag she'd eyed months before. "It'll be easier to sleep in the car now, right?" Even now, sleeping in her bed regularly again, she slept on top of the bag, using it as an extra pad just to keep it close.

Tommy got pure joy out of the camera for the brief time it lasted. He used up most of the film in a single day. The first few shots were of nothing important, but as it went on—one afternoon spent lounging at the house, just waiting for the sun to set—Tommy seemed to be trying to capture that which he especially wanted to preserve: Jesus, in any moment he would be still and friendly enough to let him.

She didn't get to see them until the night of her interrogation, but Daisy recognized the ones of Jesus in the kitchen, making a sandwich, driving the junker, sitting with Avia on the couch, and one a blurred swath of black hair that Daisy knew was when Jesus finally turned away and told Tommy to "put that shit away before I break it."

Avia herself was never a prominent figure in the pictures, only ever caught in the frame with the real target, Jesus, but Daisy was surprised to see that a scant handful of the pictures were of her—brushing her teeth, waiting for Avia to return from the bathroom at a diner, sitting on the front steps of the Flanders house with the wind stirring her hair.

Daisy pocketed the camera one day and never said anything. No one asked.

By the time April came, Daisy knew they were not coming back. There was a hollowing that happened inside her whenever she thought about it. She was never not thinking about it.

Two of the major news stations in Sweet Valley did an in-depth report on Emily Burns's disappearance, their second in two months. Emily would be added to a national registry of missing persons. Mr. and Mrs. Burns appeared on the screen, speaking in hushed, stilted voices. Daisy noted that Emily, to her recollection, didn't look like either of her parents. Then she promptly went outside and threw up in the backyard.

Her mother mentioned that she and Rusty were thinking about getting married. Rusty, that was his name. Daisy wanted to brain her mother with the plate of meatloaf she was struggling to eat. Instead, she calmly got up from her seat and went to bed.

She barricaded the door with her dresser for good measure.

The summer came and dipped into one long suffocating dream. The billboards of the dead girl, beloved to the media and icon to the ignorant youth, were not taken down after the story lost its punch. Whispers on the streets said that a girl further south in the state claimed the Burns identity and turned out to be a fake. The FBI would be involved soon, and they would seize the entire city in a chokehold until it coughed her up. Fliers featuring her immaculate face clogged the gutters of the valley. Avia and the boys became characters she created in her head. Emily was an unseen phantom, and Daisy could only sit and wither, wondering.

In the midst of a summer heat wave that lingered into the evening hours, Daisy fished out the items she'd guarded so jealously and buried them unceremoniously in the first lot she came to. Absentmindedly, she wondered how Jesus had kept calm while disposing of Emily, while she could hardly dig into the earth deep enough for a hole with her hands shaking as they were. She wondered what exactly had been planned during those hours it was just Avia and Jesus, and whose idea it was to leave Daisy behind. As she was heading home, she thought she heard a voice talking to her, but the noise panicked her, and she broke into a sprint.

Over the rest of the summer, she visited the spot. People saw, and she didn't notice. In the meantime, the grass grew fresh and green, the earth was warm, and the blocks were lively again well into the nighttime. The valley was lively, if not lovely, and that spring in particular seemed to buzz with an energy not seen in many seasons. Time never stopped for anyone, and Daisy felt largely indifferent. The best of her had been stolen. She would not try to be normal for anything.

"Tell me what's *wrong*." Her mother crouched over Daisy on the bed. She flinched with every movement of her mother's hand combing through her hair, catching on the snags and tugging her head forward and back. "You won't eat, you won't speak. Are you even in there? Where do you go?" Daisy did not answer. The nails scratching her scalp were all wrong; no smoker's laugh; no dirty puns; no reason to respond. Eventually her mother only looked at her as she came and went, staring after her as if checking to confirm what she was seeing.

The first month of the school season—that's when Emily's body was discovered. That's when the story of her life and demise became the city's obsession all over again. That's when Detective Martinez began the search for answers, and for Daisy.

And when she saw the headlines on the front page of the newspaper the school secretary was reading—even as she was trying to make Daisy's life difficult from the first week of the semester—she was surprised to find that she was glad. The only real inheritance Avia had left her with was guilt, a monstrous load to bear. Emily's discovery felt like the beginning of the end; it was a brand-new path leading—she hoped—toward absolution.

If Daisy set out and walked for a thousand nights, she would never find Avia again. She wasn't supposed to either. That was not part of the plan, after all. Avia insisted more than once that after all, everything that happened was according to *someone's* plan. "But not yours or mine, Daisy darling. Small potatoes, that's us."

So then why adopt her for the year they spent together? Through summer days slept straight through, from the nights spent scrapping to days languishing away in a class, waiting for the day to end, Avia and her boys had been there, keeping her fed and clothed, active and hopeful. Avia had never hinted she would leave Daisy high and dry—and if she had, Daisy would not have given her the chance.

Avia had said Daisy seemed like an easy target to others who would take advantage of her. She had believed Daisy needed looking after. She had blossomed under Avia's care and embraced her teachings, and maybe that was the problem. Daisy had killed for Avia.

Avia had looked into her face once and taken a day to let it sink in before she fled. What had Avia seen in Daisy that night? She had expected Avia to be proud, or at least grateful—here was her pupil, practicing what her leader had preached. Perhaps when she looked in Daisy's eyes she saw herself: a killer, fresh and new and terrifying.

They were getting in a car and going somewhere. Martinez might have told her directly, but she couldn't recall the words. He was no different upon returning to the interrogation room to collect her, but she was. She flinched when he reached for her arm; she stumbled as he led along. She stank of fear ,and Martinez would not stop frowning.

They stood on the curb outside the station, and that helped. It felt like a lifetime since Daisy had breathed fresh air. Her mother wasn't going to ride with them, and it was a relief. There was no guarantee she wouldn't show up later and cause a scene, and if she could, Daisy would rather have had her not come at all.

Martinez had an arm firmly wrapped around her shoulders. It was nice. She held herself perfectly still so as not to remind him she was there. They did not talk as they waited, and that was nice too. She had said more to him in those hours in that cramped room than she had ever said to anyone else.

There was one last thing, though. "You need to know that I…I'm sorry." She prayed that her words sounded genuine. "I mean it. I wish it had never happened. Any of it. I regret all of it." She swallowed, and any other words she might have said would not come.

He turned to her and drank her in with a furrowed brow. Looking up at him, Daisy suddenly thought of her father. She had never known him, and her mother never even kept pictures of him in the house. Detective Martinez didn't strike her as the type that would ever have children, and it was unfortunate.

She told herself that they would never have met at all if it hadn't been for all the nonsense—the ugliness of her life. She tried to tell herself that hers were a series of bright, illuminating moments like the movies her mother would take her to. The fast, violent, exciting times that set you alight with adrenaline. But as she looked at this tired man, and he studied her in turn, Daisy felt no sensation of power. She felt more like a witness to a fire, and she was only now expelling the smoke from her lungs. It had all been a waste. Daisy felt the sting of tears and tried to bury the emotion conjured up from her sentiment. After all this time, she was still sentimental.

The detective never actually answered her, and that may have been a blessing. But for a few moments Daisy felt a heavy, calloused hand roving over her hairline. She recognized the awkward catch of his wrist as inexperience; this was a hand that had never comforted a child. It finished its journey at the nape of her neck and squeezed once before curling carefully back around her shoulders. That was all.

ACKNOWLEDGEMENTS

Firstly, I thank God for His grace and compassion in my life. Not a day goes by that I don't count my blessings and feel grateful for all I've been given. To my grandmother, you were a much-needed show of support and positive feedback, and I thank you for giving me the encouragement I needed and urging me on. To my mother, I thank you for having more faith in me than I do myself, and I acknowledge in print that you are always right about everything in any given situation at any time. To Jonathan, you are a constant source of inspiration—and a wonderful person. And to my Uncle J, the smartest man I know, I thank you for being an excellent role model (and occasional ally against the rest of the family).

To Kayla and my friends, I thank you for your advice and help. To Tom, my project manager, the PR team, and the editorial team at TCK, I thank you from the bottom of my heart for this wonderful opportunity and all your help in making it happen. And lastly, to the individuals that the characters in this novel are based on: Your lives may not be glamorous or even peaceful, but they are deeply meaningful, and they do carry weight.

ABOUT THE AUTHOR

Being a Texas Panhandle native, having grown up in a house filled with books and been given the freedom to let her imagination roam free, Karlianna Voncil dreamed of writing a story that showcased both the prairie lands and the indomitable spirit of its people. She has lived in and traveled to various states and countries across two continents, but still calls Texas home. She and her immediate family share an acre with a small farm. While her recent accomplishments include earning her Master of Arts in Education, she is currently pursuing a career in teaching at the collegiate level and her doctoral degree. She is a voracious reader and was first published at the age of eight. This is her first novel.

CONNECT WITH KARLIANNA VONCIL

If you would like to know more, please visit:

www.karliannavoncil.com

Facebook:

www.fb.me/karliannavoncil

Facebook group:

Karlianna Voncil Books

GET BOOK DISCOUNTS & DEALS

Get discounts and special deals on our bestselling books at

www.TCKpublishing.com/bookdeals